CONTROLLING HERITAGE

A CONTROL SERIES NOVEL

Anna Edwards

Dear Sara,

Step into the

light!

Anna

Edwards

x

www.AuthorAnnaEdwards.com

This is a work of fiction. Names, characters, places, and incidents are a product of the author's imagination. Locales and public names are sometimes used for atmospheric purposes. Any resemblance to actual people, living or dead, or to businesses, companies, events, institutions, or locales is completely coincidental.

Warning: This book contains sexually explicit scenes and adult language and may be considered offensive to some readers. This book is for sale to adults only, as defined by the laws of the country in which you made your purchase.

Disclaimer: Please do not try any sexual practice, without the guidance of an experienced practitioner. Neither the publisher nor the author will be responsible for any loss, harm, injury or death resulting from the use of the information contained in this book.

Cover Design by www.CharityHendry.com
Logo Design by Charity Hendry
Edits by Tracy Damron-Roelle
Formatting by Charity Hendry

Controlling Heritage/ Anna Edwards -- 1st ed.
ISBN 978-1973830597

Dedication:

To the two people that I give my heritage, my son and daughter. I know that you are not allowed to read this until you are at least eighteen but know that mummy loves you both so much. ALWAYS.

CONTENTS

Grayson

"Why don't you come here and sit on my face?" Grayson lowered his leather pants and pulled out his rigid cock; the tip was already dripping with pre-cum. "And you two can suck my dick." Blonde 'one' dropped her lacy thong down her slender legs and straddled over his body and slid up to his face. He could smell how ready she was for him. It was a pretty cunt, but you could tell that it got a regular fucking. But then that was what these girls were for. Brought in to satisfy his basic needs and to get off on the fact they had a movie star's dick inside them. Basic human instinct really. He was always working so didn't have a chance to find a date on his own, and any woman he did meet...well he could never be sure they wanted him for Grayson Moore the actor or person. It was a downside to the career that he loved doing.

"How do you like to be sucked, Master Grayson?"

Blonde 'two' inquired, while twisting her hand up his shaft.

"Show me what you know, and I'll tell you if it is wrong."

He was jaded. Everyone liked to play the submissive since Fifty Shades of Grey, but very few had their heart in it. He wanted a real submissive. Blonde 'two' flicked her tongue over the tip of his cock. He wasn't as hard as he should be. That would make for good reading in the online gossip pages these girls used to discuss how good an actor was in bed. Yes, such things did exist. He better up his game and get his head on straight. The last thing he needed was to be labelled a dud in the sack.

"Take me deeper. I want to feel the back of your throat."

"I don't know if I can." She twilled in her bimbo's voice.

"You're so big."

"Then move aside and let your friend try. You can suck my balls instead." She pouted and her friend, blonde 'three', eagerly took over. She had his cock in her mouth and at the back of her throat in a matter of seconds. Blonde 'one' wiggled her hips against his chin. He smacked her fat injected backside.

"I say when you get off babe, not you. Spread those legs further."

She gratefully obliged, and he dragged his tongue up the length of her slit and drove it into her hole. Maybe he could get into this. There was nothing like a juicy pussy to make everything right in the world. His hands slid up her body to grab a handful of her breasts. As expected they were rock hard. Un-natural.

"Fuck this." He lifted blonde 'one' up and threw her unceremoniously on the floor. Blonde 'three' paused midway down his dick. Her scarlet lipstick smudged over her face. "Get off me and get lost."

"What?" The sound of Blonde 'three' reverberated around his rapidly shrinking dick.

"But your PA promised us five thousand dollars if we spent the night with you." Realising her mistake, blonde 'two' made a rapid retreat to her clothes.

"He did what?"

"He pays us to fuck you."

"And I will pay you the same to get the FUCK out of here. Double, if you get out in the next two minutes." This time he pushed blonde 'three' off the bed and stepped over blonde 'one' who was still leg's akimbo on the floor. He yanked his jeans off a chair and put them on. A Rolling Stone's t-shirt was whipped over his head in seconds. His sneakers were next; he couldn't be bothered to tie the laces so just slid into them. Without so much as a glance over his shoulder at the naked, medically enhanced Barbie's in his luxury trailer, he slammed the door on the way out.

"Jared?" He bellowed at the top of his voice. The set was

a hive of activity, but everyone stopped and looked at him.

"Grayson." The slimy git of a PA appeared from up the director's arse. He was obviously butt licking again.

"You're fired." Grayson pulled back his fist and sent it flying into the shocked ex-PA's face.

CHAPTER ONE

Sophie

"James, I can't believe you've put me forward for this." Sophie moaned into her iPhone.

"Suck it up sis and get on with it. If you stay working for me forever, we are going to end up killing each other."

"You know I hate you right now." She rolled her eyes at big brother over the FaceTime call.

"Love you too. You'll kill it."

"I'm so nervous." She worried.

"He's a movie star. How hard can being his PA be? It's not as though he does anything of importance." James responded peevishly.

"Given his last PA is suing him for an assault that is what I'm worried about."

"His last PA was a complete dick. I'd been telling him for years to get rid of him. The assault case will disappear. Matthew is working on it." James winked at her.

"That doesn't make me any less nervous."

"Get out of the car, Sophie Isabella North and go do what you're good at. Sort that man out." He frowned.

"Thank you for getting this job for me."

"Not a problem. Phone me in the morning, UK time not LA time. I don't want you calling in the middle of the night."

"Night. Sleep well." She blew a kiss to her brother over the screen

"Night." He waved at her.

Sophie pressed the end button, and her billionaire brother disappeared. She thought a call with him might have relaxed her a little, but it hadn't. Her palms were sweating, and she developed a nervous tick in her eye.

She'd been in Los Angeles for a week now preparing for her new role. Since she could remember, she'd always been a part of James' building company helping out where she could, but a secretary was not what she wanted to do. When her brother suggested the role of personal assistant to the world famous actor, Grayson Moore, she jumped at the chance, but now that she was over five thousand miles from her family, it didn't seem like she'd made the best choice.

She opened the door of her rental car and slid her long legs out of it. She was wearing her favourite Victoria Beckham cut out back dress. It was a vibrant red, which matched her brunette hair and tanned skin. She especially liked the zip all the way up the back of the dress. It gave her that sexy edge. Mind you, it was probably a mistake to wear this dress given Grayson Moore's reputation.

"Miss North?" A security guard greeted her at the gate.

"Yes." She replied

"Mr Moore is currently out running. He asked me to show you to the pool area. He has everything set up there for your meeting. I will arrange for your car to be parked inside the grounds."

"Thank you." She smiled sweetly.

She followed the guard, noticing the modern mansion with a high vaulted ceiling and acres of glass. She was used to properties of this size, but James had a flair for antiques. It was a change to see minimalism in play. Well, minimalism except for the occasional picture of odd symbols. It wasn't a case that she needed to work. James would look out for her. It was a matter of her wanting to find her own place in the world and achieve something for herself.

Her breath caught when she saw the view from Grayson's pool area. The infinity pool stretched out to encompass the Pacific Ocean; formal gardens surrounded an outside kitchen and bar. The gardens were covered in succulents not plants, such as roses that she would expect to see in England. As she found later, there was even more to the mansion with an enormous grand foyer and a drive-through garage with its own breathtaking view of the area. There was even a window from a basement room looking into the depths of that infinity-edge swimming pool, also bathrooms with heated toilets, which also act as high-end bidets with cleaning and blow-drying services

However, this was her first sight of any of it, and the pool was fantastic.

'Wow' was the only word she could think of to describe it.

"It's the reason I bought this place." The deep American voice had her spinning on her Louboutin. Her breath caught again. Grayson Moore stood in front of her. He was topless, and his muscular chest glistened with a fine sheen of sweat. His marbled thighs rippled in tight shorts. She opened her mouth to speak, but the bulge in his shorts caught her attention. It hardened; she shuddered in desire before forcing her eyes to look up into his face. His lip was curled in a knowing smirk. He pulled a towel off a chair and wrapped it around his waist. She wanted to slap herself. He probably thought she was an airhead, standing there opening and closing her mouth like a fish.

"I...err."

"Drink?" He asked

"Please." She scrambled for a reply.

"Throat dry."

"Yes." She squeaked.

"Sit." He commanded.

She sat down on the nearest chair immediately.

She could hear him chuckle to himself. Come on Sophie. Get it together.

A butler appeared, as if by magic, with two bottles of iced water. He went to put the water beside her, but Grayson took it from him. The Butler retreated. Grayson unscrewed the lid and held it to her lips.

"Drink."

She obeyed.

"Good." He placed the bottle on the table beside her and opened his own. She watched his throat muscles working to swallow every gulp. She needed more water, maybe a cold shower? The pictures in the magazines and the films didn't do justice to just how good-looking Grayson Moore was in the flesh, especially when he was showing so much of it. His features were symmetrical perfection, and even his hair, wet with perspiration, looked like it had been coiffed for hours. Now she understood why he topped so many eligible bachelor lists.

"Did you read through all the documentation I sent you?" Grayson asked.

"I did." She found her voice, the one that made her sound like an adult, not a drooling toddler. "I brought the signed copies of the non-disclosure contract that you requested. James had his solicitors read through it."

"I expect nothing less from your brother. He's an astute businessman."

"He did have an appendix added to it. He wanted you to sign a non-disclosure for anything that I may mention to you about him. I told him that it wouldn't be needed, but he insisted."

"And that is why your brother is known as a tough negotiator in the business world. He even covers his ass with long-time friends like me." He laughed.

Grayson placed his bottle of water down and took a seat on the chair opposite her. "I'll sign the contract and have his sent back to him later."

"Thank you. I know it's not normal. But he did ask that you fax him a signed copy immediately". She squirmed slightly having to say this to her new boss, but she knew what her brother was like when thinking about his business empire.

"Don't worry."

"Where would you like me to start?" She asked.

"Have you reviewed my itinerary for the next few weeks." They were both sitting, looking out over the pool to the hills of Hollywood.

"I have. There are a few bits that I'm not sure on the timing of, but we can look into it when I've learnt a bit more about how things work here in LA."

"Perfect. That's enough work talk for the moment. Do you fancy some breakfast?"

The butler appeared again. Seriously, was he telepathically linked to Grayson somehow?

"Fruit, Miss North?"

Her tummy rumbled. She was unable to eat anything this morning due to her nerves. Now, she found herself relaxing, and she was getting hungry.

"What are you having?" She asked Grayson.

"Bacon and Eggs. After a run, I require something a bit more substantial."

She bit her lip.

"Would it rude to ask if I could get some Pancakes? I think they have become a weakness of mine."

"Not at all Miss." The butler smiled and retreated to wherever he materialised.

"Well, you can tell you are new to LA. It is novel to see a woman actually request something with carbohydrates."

"Sorry, should I have just had the fruit?" she winced.

"Not at all. I will make sure pancakes are ready for you whenever you have breakfast here."

"I think I really would stand out in LA if I ate pancakes every day."

They both laughed. She noticed Grayson had a beautiful smile. It warmed her heart with its pure nature.

"It's refreshing to find a woman whose curves are natural. Don't ever change that. Look. I'm going to be honest with you about why I fired my last PA."

"The rumours said that he was stealing from you, and you punched him on set."

"I punched him; that part is true, but he was not stealing from me. He wanted to take me along a different direction in my career than I wanted to go. And when I say career I mean reputation."

Their food arrived, and they quieted, while it was served. The pancakes were massive and covered in strawberries and cream. She would need a good run later.

"What do you mean a different direction?" She popped a mouthful in after she finished speaking. Her stomach was telling her that her throat had been cut.

"He wanted me to become more entrenched on the action hero side, not only in films but reputation as well."

"The womaniser."

"You've done your research."

"Actually, Matthew Carter presented me with a file. I just read it."

"Sounds like him. One day, I'm going to get a file on him." He took a mouthful of his bacon and eggs. They smelled delicious.

"You didn't like that reputation? I thought that helped build the franchise and made you famous?"

"Would you like the reputation of being a slut?"

"It's a bit different between men and women. You would have the reputation as a stud not a whore."

"I don't mind having the reputation of being a stud but not when the woman that give it to me are sluts. The reason I punched my PA is that he offered five thousand dollars, of my money, to three women of scant morals to make sure I got off."

"Sounds like a nice man. I can see why you punched him." She rolled her eyes.

"I will have to buy him off to get him to go away, and it sickens me that I have to give him money. I never asked for those women, but for a long time, I accepted them. I was as bad as he." He placed his knife and fork down before rubbing his fingers through his hair. "I left a lot of my culture behind; I betrayed it."

"Your Native American roots?" Grayson was an Indian, the type who wore feathers on a crown and danced around a fire in Westerns but were now often clever business people. It wasn't always obvious from looking at him as he'd inherited a lot of his British mother's features.

"Yes, they mean a lot to me, and I've betrayed them in many ways. I want to get back to them, but I also want to keep true to certain aspects of myself."

"What do you mean?"

Grayson put down his knife and fork.

"Now is probably not the time to talk of this. It's probably getting a little in deep for a first day." He tried lightening the mood with a chuckle, but she could tell that there was something deeper to his thoughts. "I've got a documentary being filmed back in my Navajo lands in a few weeks. We can discuss it more then."

"If that makes you happy." She finished her last mouthful and put the cutlery together on the plate. "I'm not sure I feel like work after that, but I better get started."

"I hope you find me a good boss. I know the reputation that I come with probably makes it a worrying prospect, but I would like to think that I can be kind."

"I'm sure everything with be fine." She gave him her most reassuring smile. He reached out and touched her hand. A spark of electricity shot up her arm. She pulled her hand away and got abruptly to her feet. "I'll call if I need anything."

She knew he had an office for her to work in, so headed back inside. The heat of his eyes burned into her back; he was watching her. It couldn't be helped; she turned back and met his eyes. Was there such a thing as an instant attraction, because there was certainly some strange mojo going on right now. This was going to be an interesting job to say the least.

CHAPTER TWO

Grayson

"When you get there, you'll be greeted the Mayor of Los Angeles, and he will direct you to where you make your mark in the concrete. He is the emcee for the event. He is new mayor as the position was vacant for many years. There will be several other dignitaries from the Chamber of Commerce as well. I'll tell you their names before you shake their hands." Grayson was trying to listen to Sophie tell him about what would happen during the ceremony to put his star on the Hollywood walk of fame, but she had on another tight dress that showed off all her curves. It was rather distracting. Maybe he should have a discussion with her about suitable attire when around him. It is hard to be erect most of the time when she was around. A black trash bag should be okay. But then, it probably didn't help that he hadn't had any naked time with a woman since the three blondes' incident. Time to get his head in the game.

"Do you have a towel for afterward?" Grayson asked.

"Of course. Wouldn't want you all dirty, now, would we." Sophie replied.

She can dirty me up at any time. Fuck. His mind was straight back in the gutter again.

"Are you alright Grayson? You look a little flushed."

"Just a hot day in LA."

"It is. So different from the UK, I'm going to need to go shopping again. Most of my clothes from England are jumpers. You don't need them here."

"I can have a personal shopper come around the house later if you want?"

"You don't need to do that. I can do a "Pretty Woman" act on Rodeo Drive."

"I think your brother may have you on the first flight home if you wore a hooker outfit in Beverly Hills." After he, himself, peeled her out of the outfit and licked every inch of her body. Damn it, he was going to hell. He couldn't seem to have a decent thought.

Her cheeks pinked. "I didn't mean that part."

"I know." He interrupted just as the car pulled to a stop outside East town on Hollywood Boulevard.

"After you Mr famous movie star."

He got out the car to the flashing of paparazzi bulbs. The screams of his young fans grew to a crescendo. "Grayson, Grayson." They all chanted, "show us your muscles." Later, he mouthed at them, and a couple took a swoon. Despite the chaos of the situation, he enjoyed the admiration that he got for his work.

"Mr Moore, it's a pleasure to meet you." The mayor held his hand out, and Grayson confidently shook it.

"Likewise. This is my assistant, Sophie North."

"We've spoken already. A pleasure to meet you as well, Miss North."

She shook the mayor's hand. He was younger than Grayson expected for a mayor and he couldn't help feel a pang of jealously as Sophie gave the mayor a seductive smile. That was his smile. Jesus, was he going insane? He wasn't this type of man. He wanted Sophie in his bed, and he wasn't going to stop till he had her.

The emcee started his introductions, and the ceremony began. He placed his hands into the cement and signed his name. That would be turned into a plaque and put elsewhere at a later date. Next was to reveal his star. Since he'd been a child on the plains of Monument Valley, he'd wanted to be a movie star. He didn't envision action films; he liked the old cowboy and westerns that they shot around his home. He'd love to do one of them, but also he loved drama. Unfortunately, he was told that with his looks he was better suited to action movies. That didn't mean that now he'd made it he couldn't do what he wanted. This was what his trip back to Monument Valley would allow him to do.

He pulled the cover back off his star, and the paparazzi went mad again. He flashed his perfect smile and enabled them to get all the shots they needed. When the ceremony finished, he spent some time talking to fans and signing autographs. Sophie approached him.

"Sorry, Grayson. We have to get going now. Your lunch meeting is scheduled for half an hour." Sophie pointed out.

"Thank you." He signed a final few autographs then placed his hand on the small of Sophie's back. It was a natural gesture, and he didn't think anything of it until the cameras around them started flashing.

"Are you two dating?" A reporter's voice called out. Sophie realised his mistake and pulled herself away.

"Sophie is my personal assistant; I'm just a gentleman." He winked at the reporter. Out of the corner of his eye, he couldn't help but notice Sophie look timidly down at the ground. There was a look of regret on her face. Was it from the loss of his touch or the mistake he'd made? They walked in silence to the car, and that awkward reticence continued until they reached the restaurant for his meeting with a possible co-star for his new project.

"Tessa is already inside apparently. She arrived five minutes ago. The maître d escorted her to her seat and provided her with champagne. I'll wait in the car for you." She didn't look at him when she spoke, simply rifled through a folder of papers that she had on her lap.

"You're not joining us?" He asked.

"I thought you would be better able to sell your ideas to Tessa without me there." She replied not taking her eyes off the papers.

"Oh. I would like you there though." The words left his mouth before he really had a chance to think about what he was saying. She looked panicked. "You've read the script and know it back to front like me. You can give a woman's point of few."

She nodded happily. "Alright. I'll join you."

"Thank you. Sophie, is everything ok?"

"Just a little homesick." She lied. He saw that flash quickly over her eyes.

He couldn't help it. He took her face and gently brought it up to meet his. Her eyes could not look away from him.

"You just lied to me. If you were mine, I would punish you."

Her breath hitched. He'd heard it.

"Do you know what that would entail?" His voice was low and commanding.

"Yes." She expectantly whispered.

The car door opened, and she was able to break the spell that he had her trapped in. He'd never seen someone scramble out of a car so quickly and still managed to maintain dignity and pose. He followed and strode past her.

"This is not over." He pointedly whispered.

The maître d showed them to the table, which his vivacious actress friend was sitting at. She tapped out a message on her phone but placed it down when she saw them.

"Grayson, Darling." She stood and flung her arms around him, kissing him feverishly on the cheeks.

"Tessa. It is good to see you again."

"And you. I'm sure those arm muscles of yours grow every time I see you. I bet you could bench press me with just the one arm now."

"I wasn't far off in Renegade Two." He retorted.

"No, you weren't actually." Her eyes looked behind him at Sophie. "And who is this lovely lady?" She winked.

"Tessa, this is Sophie North, my personal assistant." He introduced Sophie.

"Just personal assistant? She is far too gorgeous for that."

"Just personal assistant." He growled.

Tessa repeated her over the top greeting with Sophie. He couldn't help but notice that she lingered a little longer with her hold though. He and Tessa had become good friends while filming Renegade Two. Unfortunately, her character died toward the end of it, and she hadn't been in any more of the movies. They had had so much fun. Especially one night at a club when they had both topped a submissive. Tessa was a switch but preferred to only top women. She would have instantly sensed Sophie's passive nature and be interested in the dynamic of their relationship. Even if it was technically still classed as a working one.

He assisted both ladies to sit and handed them menus. The restaurant was one of his favourites, because it served a lot of Native American dishes. Home cooked food presented in a 'posh' way.

Sophie coughed

"Is everything alright?"

He looked over to her.

"The menu's a little bit alien to me."

Tessa leant forward.

"Don't worry, darling, the first time I came here, I had no idea what I was eating. Grayson, why don't you order for Sophie."

There was no mistaking the meaning behind her tone of voice. As a Master, he wanted a twenty-four-seven submissive. That would mean he would order food for her.

"I'm sure I can explain the menu to Sophie, and she can decide what she wants to eat herself." He frowned at Tessa. She just sat there with a smug smile on her face.

"No, that is fine. Please choose for me, Grayson. I don't have any allergies, and I like most foods except for mushrooms. They are the devil's food." She even stuck out her tongue and gagged at the mention of them. He couldn't help but laugh.

"Mushrooms starter followed by main mushroom course and mushroom ice cream for dessert. How does that sound?"

"Like I might throw up in your lap?"

"Maybe I'll get you Goat's milk pancakes, roasted mutton, and then, yucca fruit salad for dessert. How does that sound?"

"Much better." She gave him her cheeky smile. That was

better to see. Shame when he turned to Tessa she just raised a knowing eyebrow. He was screwed and not on the level that he wanted.

The lunch meeting went well, and he convinced Tessa to join them in the new project. She was to play his love interest. Sophie excused herself to go to the bathroom while he paid. Tessa leant forward on the table.

"So?"

"So what?" He tried to play dumb.

"She is perfect. Where did you find her?"

"She is an exceptional PA; yes, I agree." He signed the bill and handed it back to the waiter.

"Don't play dumb with me Grayson. I know you too well." Tessa tapped her long talon fingernails on the table.

"Back off Tessa. She is my PA. That is all."

"You want more?" She asked.

"PA." He replied in frustration.

"She's a submissive."

"She is the sister of a good friend of mine."

"She's a twenty-four-seven submissive." Tessa was chuckling now.

He placed his hand on his head and ran his fingers through his hair.

"I know." He almost cried.

"Have you spoken to her about it?"

"No."

"She is what you have been looking for, for years?"

"You don't have to remind me." He pushed his chair sharply back and stood. "Just leave it, please, Tessa."

"Is everything alright?" Sophie was behind him.

"Yes." He answered a little too quickly.

"Tessa?"

"Everything is fine, darling. Just teasing Grayson here."

"I took the liberty of requesting both our cars. They should be out the front."

"You are a God send. If you ever tire of Grayson, I would love a new PA."

"I'll bare that in mind." Sophie giggled. "It was lovely to meet you, Tessa. I look forward to seeing you again soon."

"The feeling is mutual." He watched both women hug and then stepped forward to embrace Tessa himself.

"Thank you for agreeing to the project."

"No worries. I'm looking forward to it."

"I'm sorry for shouting." Sophie walked off in the direction of the entrance to check on the cars.

"I'm sorry for bringing it up, but Grayson, hear this though. Don't waste this opportunity. It will be your biggest regret."

He looked toward Sophie as she shook the hand of the maître d.

"I know."

CHAPTER THREE

Sophie

They set off from Grayson's LA home early that morning to fly to the private airport close to the Navajo lands. The Jeep Grand Cherokee that waited for them was brand new. Sophie felt a little guilty that its shiny exterior was probably going to be ruined in a few hours by the sandy landscape, which surrounded them. It might be barren, but it was beautiful. A terracotta red, it shimmered in the hot sun. Boy, was it hot!

"Make sure you keep drinking." Grayson motioned toward a bottle of water, which had been placed in the car for them. She had arranged a driver for them, but Grayson had stated that he wanted to do the driving, so they travelled alone. His bodyguard travelled in a car behind, even though he said he didn't need him either. She wasn't going to take any risks on her watch. The bodyguard had been told to stay back and not disturb Mr Moore. Just keep watch.

"And there was me thinking LA was hot." She fanned herself with a piece of paper.

"Told you to pack lightweight clothing." He countered.

"I am glad you told me to change out of the designer dress and just put on a maxi dress. I would be melting already if I didn't."

"See, Grayson knows best." She saw a big cheeky smile spread all over his face. They developed a great working relationship where they spent most of the time teasing each other.

"Sometimes. I'm your PA remember. I'm the one who knows best about where you have to be and when."

"That is very true."

The smile turned to a fake frown. "I'd probably still be

back in bed scratching my head wondering how I was going to re-arrange my flight if you hadn't have set my alarm this morning."

"See, talented PA."

"Very smart." The words rolled off his tongue with velvety innuendo.

He had backed off since the day of his star unveiling, and she was a lot more relaxed around him. She knew that she had feelings for him. Every day that she spent with him, she found something else that he did that she liked. She just couldn't risk a relationship with him though.

They pulled through the gate of Grayson's ancestral home. They would be staying at a hotel tonight, as it was easier, but he still wanted to see his parents. His house was nothing special. She learnt that he offered to upgrade his parents on so many different occasions, but each time, they refused. They like the simplicity of the native way of living. In the four walls, they had all they needed. That didn't mean that they weren't the best dressed on the reserve, apparently. His mother had a weakness for fashion and jewellery. She made her own but always made sure she purchased the best stones to do it with.

"Yá'át'ééh."

"Giní" A woman ran out of the netted front door. Grayson was over six foot in height, but the woman was only five foot so looked so strange next to him. He picked her up and swung her around in his arms.

"Shimá." She'd done some basic research on the Navajo language and knew that this meant mother. So this woman was Grayson's mum. She saw it now. She had the same eyes as he, although his colouring was purely native.

"We weren't expecting you for another few hours."

"My PA is a slave driver and wanted to get travelling early, so we can scout out some locations for the filming."

His mother peeked behind his shoulder

"And is this beautiful lady your PA?"

"She is. Shimá, please meet Sophie."

Sophie stepped forward and offered her hand to his mother, but she grabbed her and pulled her into her arms.

"We don't stand on ceremony here, girl. We give big hugs."

"I think everyone I've met in America, so far, does. I think we British folks have far too much of a stiff upper lip."

"No, my mother is just a very huggy person." Grayson placed his arm around his mother's shoulder."

"Be nice Giní or there will be no cactus pudding for you."

"Giní?" She'd heard that word twice, now. It wasn't one she recognised.

"It means Hawk in my native language. That is my spirit animal."

"Suits you. Always watching."

"You better believe it, Miss North."

"I wondered why you were preparing so much food?" A younger well-set woman strutted up the pathway like she owned the place. "Brought another one of your LA slaves for us to supposedly fawn over, brother?"

"Déélgai." Grayson's mother admonished. "Sophie is Grayson's personal assistant."

"And what exactly does she assist him with, I wonder."

"Swan, if you got nothing nice to say them, maybe you could crawl back under your rock and allow me and my friend to have a nice dinner with mom and dad."

She was named after a swan; that was a big irony. She was nothing like the graceful and beautiful bird. From the death stare vibes coming off Grayson, she wondered if the young girl's heart was made of pure venom.

"You think I'd actually sit at a table with someone as filthy as you and your whore. Not likely." A bead of sweat appeared on Grayson's temple. He was controlling his rage, but he was reaching the end of what even he could take. She'd seen him explode once since she'd been in LA, and it hadn't been pretty. She wasn't really in the mood for a repeat.

"Do you have a habit of insulting all guests that come to visit your mother or is it just me, because I'm white?" She'd had just about enough insults to last her a lifetime. She wasn't stupid. She knew what this woman meant by her comments.

"Don't flatter yourself, princess. I couldn't care less what the colour of your skin is. It's the what you let this man do to you that concerns me."

"What pay my salary to organise his schedule? I personally can't see anything wrong with that."

"I think I mean more the fact that he ties you up and beats you up."

"Enough Swan." Grayson's mother stepped up this time. "I will come over tonight to see you, but for now, I want to have a pleasant lunch with my son and his friend. Leave."

"I've no idea why you even still associate with him. He turned his back on us. You'll regret it one day." With that final retort, Swan left.

"I'm sorry you had to witness that, Sophie. I'm afraid my daughter doesn't agree with my son's choice of occupation. Hopefully, one day, we will be able to build some sort of bridge between them."

"It's not a problem. Please, Mrs Moore. Don't think anything more of it." She reassured.

"Thank you, dear. Grayson why don't you show Sophie around a bit. I'll have your dinner ready in two hours. I know you wanted to look at locations for your film."

"Will do. Love you, mom."

"And you." Grayson looked pensively at the floor, as his deflated mother walked back into the house. The elation of their arrival replaced with worry and strain.

"It's not because of your film career is it?" Sophie asked.

"Sorry?"

He looked up at her.

"It's because of your dominant and submissive beliefs?"

He nodded.

"Let's go and look at the locations. I want to know more about where you grew up." She held out her hand to him. He took it. She led them back to the car.

"Take me to see the monuments."

"Sophie."

She put a finger to his lips.

"You know my brother's past."

"Yes."

"Give me time."

CHAPTER FOUR

Grayson

The journey to Monument Valley was made in relative silence, just the sound of the radio for company. Sophie spent most of her time looking out the window, lost in her thoughts. Her brother was one of his friends. He was beaten and scarred for life because of his beliefs in the BDSM world. Sophie was a teenager when it happened. It must have left its scars. She had her left hand on her lap as she sat. He reached out and wrapped his fingers around hers. She turned her head and looked up at him. There were unshed tears in her eyes. Painful memories were flooding her mind. He squeezed her hand, and she smiled. They made the rest of the journey this way. Hand in hand.

"I can drive around the resort if you want, or we can take one of the tours. What would you prefer?"

"I would actually like to take the tour if that is alright. Do something proper touristy. But won't you get recognised?"

He nodded to the cap and sunglasses in the back. "I should be fine."

"The ever-faithful disguise." She laughed.

"It hides a multitude of sins."

"If only it were that easy." She quietened again. They pulled up to the tour stop. He put on the hat and glasses

"No more frowns. Come on." He hopped out the car with a spring, came around to her side, and helped her out with an over the top theatrical bow.

"What was that for?" She looked at him quizzically.

"To see that smile back on your face."

"You're an idiot." She rolled her eyes.

"And you love it."

"Hawk?"

A voice called out from behind them.

"Wolf." Grayson replied.

His friend approached, and they bear hugged, slapping each other hard on the back. Wolf had been his best friend for years.

"What are you doing here? I hope you're not going to start a stampede, Mr famous movie star."

"I hope not as well, hence the disguise."

"Yeah. Not that convincing mate. I saw through it in a minute."

"Yeah, but your ugly mug spent most of its life looking at my stunningly handsome face, so it should recognise it."

"I see you haven't acquired modesty yet." Wolf shook his head.

"Never." They bear hugged again.

"Who's the chick?" Wolf flicked his head in acknowledgement of Sophie.

"Wolf, this is Sophie, my PA and friend. She wants to do the tour, if you can squeeze us in somewhere." Without thinking about, it he put his arm around Sophie and brought her close to him. It was a protective gesture, but it was also a keep your hands-off warning.

"Of course we can. Come on. I'll get you on the next bus. Follow me."

They followed Wolf through the sea of people to the front of the queue. Several grumbled curses under their breath. Grayson dropped his hand from Sophie's shoulder to her hand and gripped it tightly.

"If they only knew who they were complaining at." Sophie giggled into his ear.

"Don't give away hints." He winked at her then helped her into a rundown bus, which they used for the tour.

"I'm so excited about this.

The bus started up. He learnt from experience to hold on, but Sophie hadn't. She went flying at the first bump and landed across his lap.

"I'm sorry." She pushed up, and her hand grazed his

groin. He swelled within his jeans. She blushed.

"I should have warned you; it's a little bumpy."

"I'll be sure to hold on, this time."

She quickly tried to scramble back to her her side of the seat, but he placed his arm around her shoulders and brought her into his chest.

"I'll keep you safe." The words were loaded heavily with his meaning. He wanted to protect her in so many different ways.

"I know." She whispered back to him before focusing her attention on the 'Mittens' and buttes. The magnificent, monumental sandstone landforms seemed to connect the ground to the sky. This was where the ancestral spirits of the Navajo Nation were infused with the rugged landscape, which seemed so alien, yet so, oh so, familiar due to its constant use in Hollywood films.

The trip lasted no more than half an hour. He watched Sophie's excited face the entire time. She was happy. He always felt that she held a little something of herself back around him. She wasn't now though. She felt the magic of his ancestral lands. He knew it.

He helped her from the bus. She didn't drop his hand but held it tightly as they walked around the booths, which some of the Indian women had set up. They sold wares, trinkets, sandstone pictures, and some beautiful jewellery, made the traditional way.

"How much is this, please?" Sophie picked up a silver bangle with a natural turquoise stone.

"That'll be ten dollars," the lady selling it replied.

"I'll take it please." She reached into her strap over bag to produce her purse.

"I'll pay." He placed his hand over hers.

"You don't have to." She replied.

"I want to."

"Thank you." She smiled and placed the bangle on her wrist. He handed over a twenty and told the seller to keep the change. They resumed holding hands while returning to the car.

"Grayson." Sophie stopped at the door of the car.

"Yes?" he cocked his head her way in reply.

She went up on her tiptoes and pressed a soft kiss to his cheek. It warmed his body, especially when she lingered close. "Thank you for today."

"It's not over yet. We have dinner and then let's go to the hotel."

CHAPTER FIVE

Sophie

The words 'it's not over yet' hung heavily in the air during the forty-minute drive to the Desert Rose Inn, after a fabulous dinner with Grayson's parents. She was sure she should've been looking out the window as the sights, but the true meaning of those words left her confused. It hadn't been the words necessarily; it was the way he said them. The purpose behind them. She was probably reading too much into it, and he simply meant to sleep. She was so stupid. Yes, he was implying to sleep. Time to focus on the landscape; she scolded herself.

"We're almost there." A few moments later, they pulled up to the modern looking, wooden lodge hotel. It was beautifully set against the red landscape. "It's not a fancy hotel; I'm afraid. We don't have a lot of them around here, but I like its quirky style. Reminds me a lot of home."

"I'm sure it is fine. If not, I'll get my brother to build one here for next time we visit." Grayson helped her from the car, and a porter ran out to take their luggage. The middle-aged manager of the hotel appeared and shook Grayson's hand warmly.

"It's a pleasure to have you at our hotel, again, Mr Moore."

"It's good to be back. This is my PA, Sophie North." He pushed her forward, so she could shake hands.

"I believe we spoke when I booked the hotel."

"We did. Such a beautiful accent and an English rose to match."

"Flattery, just what I like." She replied with a smile.

"I've put you in the family suite. It should be quieter there. We have a conference going on, so most of the King rooms are booked. Everything that you requested is in the chamber already, if you'd like to follow me." They followed the slightly greying man through the grounds to a small log cabin.

The second that the door was opened, she knew why Grayson liked this place. The stunning rooms were furnished just as she would have imagined. Colourful and cosy, like an Indian chief's headdress. It was a piece of Grayson. His flair painted on the walls of a log cabin.

"Do you like it?"

"I love it. How did you find this place?"

"I used to stay at my parent's when I visited, but with my sister's attitude, it became more difficult. This place was recommended, and I've stayed here every time since."

Grayson stepped away and tipped the manager and concierge. She kicked her shoes off and padded through the entranceway into the kitchen. Opening the fridge and pouring two glasses of chilled water, she set them down on the counter. Grayson came into the room and drank his in one long swallow. She couldn't help but watch his throat working as he did so. It was one of her favourite things to do. It was so masculine in its motion. She turned away before she dribbled her desire down her chin.

"I'm going to make a few phone calls. Check the schedule for tomorrow."

She hurriedly picked up her bag and started for the door.

"Stop." Her body froze to the spot. Grayson's demand rendering her limbs immobile. She was a puppet, and he was pulling all the strings. "Face me." She willed her body to keep walking. She knew that if she turned around, she would be lost. She wanted him. He wanted her. "Sophie." Her bag fell to the floor, and she pivoted. Her feet caught in the straps and she stumbled. He was there to catch her. The concern in his darkening eyes boring into her.

"Tell me no." His voice wavered for a moment; his mahogany eyes continued boring into her.

"I can't."

He brought his lips down onto hers. Gentle at first then firm with passion. Demanding entry to her mouth. She opened, and he invaded her mouth with his skilful tongue. Her head was spinning. This shouldn't be happening. Her betraying body preparing itself for the pleasure it needed from the handsome man cradling it. He was her boss. She was his personal assistant. A job that required she make sure he showed up to a meeting at the right time not drop her knickers to satisfy his carnal needs. Drop her knickers. Shit. She was already planning on getting naked. It was getting hard to breath. She pressed against his chest. He pulled back, and she scrambled to the other side of the room.

"I'm sorry. I shouldn't have done that." She looked at the floor, hoping it would swallow her up. "I'll hand in my notice and find a taxi out of here."

Grayson growled. He actually growled. What the fuck! Like the domineering man he was, he prowled across the room in a few strides. He was in front of her and lifting her chin up, so their eyes met.

"Why are you so scared, my little one?"

"I'm not scared." Her reply was barely audible.

"Do you want to fuck me?" The intent in his tone went straight into her pants.

"Grayson." She pleaded.

"Answer me."

She wavered on her reply. He had her captured. She couldn't look away, even if she wanted to.

"Yes."

In a swift movement, he bent down and scooped her up into his arms. They were leaving the kitchen and entering the bedroom, before she could even whimper a protest. He laid her out on the bed like a delicate piece of china. Tender and full of affection. Then, the animal appeared again. Her dress was over her head, leaving her in just her knickers; she hadn't needed a bra with the dress. His ravenous gaze drank in her body. He licked his lips when he reached her breasts. She wasn't a virgin, but no man had ever made her skin heat the way Grayson's stare did.

"Lower your panties down those long legs of yours." Her hands went to the lace top of her black Victoria's Secret knickers. They seemed to be dropping all on their own without her even thinking about it. "Keep your eyes on me." She pulled her pants off over her feet and held them up in the air. He took them, brought them to his nose and took a long drawn out inhalation of her scent. "I'll be keeping these."

"Grayson." She squirmed on the bed, rubbing her thighs together to get friction where she so desperately needed it.

"Legs apart. You know how this works." She did. When her brother was beaten for his sexual beliefs, she did a lot of research on BDSM. Even if she hadn't known Grayson's sexual persuasion, she could just feel the essence of Dom he eluded. She opened her legs to display her glistening sex to him. She was ready.

"How many lovers have you had?" Grayson removed his t-shirt and shorts while he spoke.

"Who says I've had any?" She coyly replied. Her mind was in other places, like the muscular chest in front of her leading down to a rippled stomach and a that 'v' of promise. So much promise judging by the bulge in his designer boxers.

"I know you had at least one. The fact that you're almost salivating at what has captured your attention in my pants and not looking worried tells me that. I think we'll have your eyes on my face for now."

She grumbled while working her eyes in reverse up his body. "I've had two lovers."

"Tell me about them?"

"Seriously?" This was not what she wanted to be doing right now. She wanted his boxers off and what she suspected a massive cock pushing into her.

"I want to know everything about you, Sophie."

"Can't we just have sex and then I can tell you?"

"No."

"Damn." She pouted. "Alright, I lost my virginity at sixteen to the first ever boyfriend I had. We are school sweethearts. It was nice."

"Just nice?" He was still standing at the foot of the bed. She had to look at his face, but every now and then, his gaze would travel elsewhere on her body."

"We didn't really know what we were doing. It got better, but then we went to different university's and split up."

"Who was next?"

"A mistake." She was embarrassed by this one.

"Keep going."

"I went out with my girlfriends one night, and they set me up. I got drunk, and the guy and I had fumbled sex against a toilet wall in the pub. He zipped up afterwards and left without even saying thank you. I was so ashamed."

"When was this?"

"I was seventeen...so five years ago."

"You've not been with anyone since?"

"No. James was attacked shortly afterwards, so I swore off men and focused on my career." Those thoughts about whether she was doing the right thing suddenly flooded back.

"Stop." He demanded of her.

"Stop what?" She questioned.

Grayson climbed over her on the bed, his large frame swamping her.

"Doubting what is about to happen. I'm not going to zip up and walk away afterwards. I plan on coming inside you a lot more than once. And, it's going to be a lot more than nice."

She let out a little chuckle. "I guess you know that from your vast experience in the field of play?"

"Is that a subtle way of asking about my lovers?"

"I didn't think it was that subtle." She shrugged her shoulders.

"It's not as many as you think." And with those words, he silenced her thoughts with another kiss. His lips tasted at the corners of her mouth, travelling over her jaw and down her chin in a mixture of kisses and bites. He reached her breasts and brought his hand up to massage the left while the right was treated to the expert talents of his tongue.

"Oh God." She murmured, her voice husky with lust.

He went lower still, parting her legs with his hands to display her neatly shaven femininity. His tongue worked its magic down there as well, flicking over her clit, withdrawing it from its hood until she thought she might burst. He pressed a finger inside her, then two, stretching her out ready for him. It was all she could do to stay in her body.

"Please." She pleaded. Her hands gripped the sheets, talon nails embedding into the luxurious fabrics. She never climaxed this quickly, even when fondling herself. "I'm going to come."

"Come." He didn't need to tell her twice. She climaxed all over his tongue and fingers. So much pleasure. Fuck. She was high. Her body shuddering so violently. She started to come down, but he flicked inside her with his tongue, and up and over, she soared again.

"Grayson!" She screamed out his name. Her voice was hoarse. Her body red hot from desire but sated by his actions.

He had withdrawn his fingers from her body and was dropping his pants. When he said she didn't look scared of what was in his pants, he'd been doing himself a disservice. Now he was exposed in front of her, he was massive. The thickly veined member, with a slight curve to the left, standing proudly. He bent to ruffle in his jeans. Retrieving a condom, she watched as he covered himself.

"We will need to look into birth control and examinations. Tonight will be the only time I take you with a condom."

"You're rather confident that I will want you to take me more than once."

"How many times did you just orgasm?"

"Twice." She shrugged, the juices still trickling down her

legs reminding her of the ferocity and pleasure of both climaxes.

"Can you feel your legs?"

He had a point there. She suspected if she tried to walk she would end up in a heap on the floor.

"Put yourself inside me, and then, we'll talk."

He shook his head. "Miss North, I can already see you're going to change my life completely." He pressed a kiss to her forehead, gently easing past her swollen folds and into her warm and very welcoming pussy.

He filled her just to the edge between painful and erotically painful. Her skin inflamed, and she came again. Her head thrown back in wonderment. Gulping breaths of air swallowed down into her lungs between screams.

"Fuck. I can feel you clamping down on me. I'm going to come as well."

Grayson pulled back and thrust in hard. His balls hit her arse, and his pelvis stroked her clit. He quickened his pace, his control a feathered piece of string. She couldn't not again. Not another one. Oh yes, she could. Grayson slammed into her one last time and spilt his release into the condom. She climaxed again. A fourth time! Her spent body collapsed like a puddle of jelly on the bed. Her new lover withdrew, and she whimpered at the slight tenderness.

"Lay there and don't move."

"I don't think I could even if I wanted to."

She watched him stride off into the bathroom. He pulled the condom off his deflating cock, wrapped it in tissue and placed in the bin. He then brought a damp flannel back to her.

"Lay still. I'm going to clean you up." He placed the warm cloth between her legs and gently wiped away the evidence of their coupling.

"I can do that." She tried to take the flannel from him

"No, it is my job."

"Your job?"

"To look after you."

"I thought it was my job to take care of you. Isn't that what PA's do?"

He turned around and sighed. His shoulder slumped.

"I knew that you should have stopped me."

"I don't understand."

"I want a relationship with you."

"I want that also." She sat up on the bed and pulled the sheet over her body. A sudden chill in the air made her want to cover herself.

"I thought you knew. Knew what I'd want. Damn, I thought James would've told you." He paced away from her. His hands in his hair tugging at the ends.

"I know you're a Dom." She called after him. "I know what that means; in the bedroom, I will submit to you, and in return, you will give me lots of pleasure. I want that as well. Especially if what just happened is anything to go by. That was the best sex I've ever had."

He turned around to face her. "I don't just want you submissive in the bedroom. Sophie, I want a twenty-four-seven submissive."

CHAPTER SIX

Grayson

He'd made a big mistake. His dick had ruled his head. And there he was trying to dispel the myth that action heroes didn't have brains.

"Twenty-four-seven?"

"Yes." She sounded so confused.

"I don't understand."

Sophie had wrapped the sheet around her body, but he'd memorised every inch of it. He was getting hard again just looking at her. Time for clothes. He grabbed his trousers and pulled them on, taking a great deal of care with the zip due to his freshly re-aroused state. He padded back along the tiled floor to the bed and perched on the end.

"You're correct about what a submissive in the bedroom is. You place your trust in me to dominate you, and in turn, I'll give you everything I can. However, I want one step further than that. I don't just want to be your Master in the bedroom. I'll control all aspects of your life. I'll tell you what to wear, what to eat. I want to feed you that food. Most times, I'll have you by my side on the sofa or at a table, but if I feel you've misbehaved, I'll make you sit at my feet. I want you to give up daily control to me to know what is best for you.

She shuffled on the bed, he could tell that she was uncomfortable with his needs.

"So basically, I'll be a slave to you."

"Far from it. You'll be treated like a princess. Worshipped and adored. Respected and loved."

"But if I'm naughty, you'll make me sit in the corner like a child." She pouted. He needed to take a gamble. He could see the submissive in her. It screamed at him to be let out.

He turned his voice dark.

"Red stops everything, Amber if you feel uncomfortable, Green for happy. Do you understand?"

"What?" She scrunched her face up in confusion.

"Do you know what I mean by that." Grayson's voice was such that an answer had to be given.

She nodded.

"I have to hear the word."

"Yes." She replied.

"On your feet."

The frown adorning her face belied the decision she was making within her head. She slid from the bed; the sheets still wrapped around her like a Greek Goddess.

"Drop the sheet."

He saw her take a sharp inhalation of breath. She made no movement.

"Drop the sheet." His voice was a deep reverberating rasp.

A moment more hesitation then the white Egyptian cotton billowed to her feet.

"Good girl. I want you to stand in the corner of the room." He pointed where. "Face the wall with your hands behind your back. I'm going to go and fix us some food. You will not move until I come back. If you do, there'll be punishment." She shuddered but didn't go to the corner. "We're in the bedroom Sophie. You've stated you want to submit to me here."

"Amber."

He handed her back the sheet, and she quickly wrapped it around herself. "Talk to me."

"I'm scared. My heart and body are telling me to go and stand in that corner. To do it because I want to. I know that you will not hurt me. I don't fear that. I am afraid of others."

"Your brother's assault?" Grayson knew Sophie's brother well. He was a Dom through and through, even if he denied it now. He tried to get slightly kinky with a girlfriend, and she had her crazy brothers beat him half to death. James had had a massive angel tattoo done over the scars, but in the right light, you could still see how much he must have suffered. Ever since that day, he'd only played in clubs under pseudonyms and often masked.

"Yes." Sophie's fearful voice interjected into his reflective thoughts. "I was only seventeen when he was attacked. Sex had still been an experimental thing at that point. I already knew from my previous encounters that I needed more than was probably normal. When James was beaten, I started reading about the lifestyle. It was what I needed. The instant I read about submission, I just knew. But I couldn't do it. I was watching my brother lying there dosed up on morphine. His back was covered in stitches from how viciously he was beaten. I'll never forget the colour of his skin. It was almost like an alien from the movies. Purples, greens, blues." He reached up and wiped away a tear that tumbled down her cheek. "His wounds eventually healed. Slowly, with physio, he learnt to walk again. But his mind...James had always been so carefree; he was witty and loving, so, so loving as a brother. He'd hold me when I cried over a bad test result at school or a fight with a girlfriend on something as mundane as who was going to marry what member of N Sync. If I had bad period pains, he would bring me a hot water bottle and chocolate. It was little things, silly things. But he stopped them all. All he did was work, go to the gym, eat and sleep. He shut down. I watched the brother I love become nothing. He's still like that. I don't know if he will ever change. I know he goes to clubs to see women. I'm not stupid. I'm glad he does that, but I just want him to be happy."

He scooted around on the bed until he held her in his arms. One hand stroking her hair in comfort.

"Your brother suffered a significant trauma. I know he is working through his issues; I've seen it, but it'll take time. He's still your brother underneath; he adores you."

"But he was made what he is today because of something he believed in. Something he craved in his soul."

"You're scared that the same thing may happen to you?"

"I am. That is why I've stayed away from sex for so long. I was scared of not being able to be normal when everything in me was screaming to be dominated. With you though, I can't control it any longer. I'm conflicted."

He inhaled deeply. His beautiful girl knew what she wanted but was terrified of the consequences. Her mind and body were in a fight for superiority.

"I can't promise you that you won't be beaten for your beliefs. No matter how much I want to. But I can no more promise a homosexual, a ménage, even different religions. I'm native American. I've suffered in the world of LA because of that. I'm one of the lucky ones who have broken through despite my heritage, but not all make it. Dreams are taken away from us every day. But having those dreams is the important part. You need to have faith in what you want. Tell me little one. What does your body say it wants?"

"It's telling me to go and stand in the corner."

"And your brain?"

"That it will only lead to pain and ridicule."

"Which one do you want to win?"

She shifted and looked up at him. Her big brown eyes filled with honesty. "My heart."

It was enough to break him. He ran a finger from the top of her forehead, down her nose and to her lips. She kissed it tenderly.

"Now, here. We try. If you decide you cannot do it, we walk away tomorrow. We will both always hold our regrets, but at least we tried. You have my word that I will never speak of what happened here. I will protect you in all aspects forever.

Sophie brought her hands up to her eyes and wiped away her tears. She then pushed out of his arms and dropped the sheet. With a soft look over her shoulder at him, she walked to the corner of the room.

He let out the breath he didn't realise he'd been holding for her actions. She was beautiful, accepting the punishment. Her hand's resting gently at the top of her pert bottom were neatly entwined. Her head bowed. He brought his hand down to the fabric of jeans and rearranged his growing, hard masculinity.

"I won't be long." He tried to keep his voice low and commanding. "You're not to move or talk. I will only be in the next room. If you need me urgently, call out ha-glade. It means mine. I will come straight away. For I will always protect what is mine. You may answer me to confirm that you understand."

"Yes...yes, Master."

"Good girl."

He left the room on shaking legs and rested his forehead against a wall. He took several deep breaths to centre himself. Damn, he was so used to control, but right now, he felt wildly out of control. What was this woman doing to him? He was rock hard; his jeans would probably be leaving an imprint on his cock. She was terrified beyond belief but was still submitting to him. He had one chance to get this right, or she would be out of his life. That would be it. He would never find a more perfect mate. He would be alone for life. His heart pained at the thought of that. It took him a few minutes to quickly throw the food, which had been left for them, onto a tray. He warmed up some of the items that needed to be so then headed back to the bedroom. Sophie hadn't moved at all. She'd obeyed. He lowered his jeans as he could no longer cope with wearing them any longer. Jogging bottoms were going to be the way to go when his little one was around.

"Lower your arms to your side and turn around to face me." She did as instructed even keeping her head bowed without prompting.

"Why did I ask you stand in the corner?"

She didn't answer.

"Sophie." Had he upset her?

"Forgive me Master, but you told me I could not speak unless it was to call ha-gade" She looked up, and the sparkle in her eye showed she was playing with him.

His heart leapt. In two longs strides, he was across the room, and she was over his knee.

"You know what cheeky little submissive's get?"

"A spanking?" She said with a wink. He'd unleashed a monster. He ran his hand between her legs, she was wet. There would be time for that later. "Count me ten." He brought his hand down on her bottom in a quick smack.

"One." She squirmed.

"Still or I double it."

"Sorry, Master."

He continued his assault on her beautiful posterior. It looked rosy pink, so hot, with his hand prints on both cheeks. On the final count, he ran his finger back over her folds. She was drenched with desire.

"I think someone enjoyed her spanking. Now answer my question, and then, you can eat."

"I would rather do something else than eat."

He smacked her again. She whimpered at the shock and tried to rub her thighs together. He brought his large hand in between her legs to stop that.

She huffed. "I doubted what you wanted from me. I thought you wanted me as a slave but being a twenty-four-seven submissive is so much more and oh so pleasurable."

"Right answer."

He brought his thumb up against her clit. It took no more than a few seconds of stroking before she came violently in his arms. He held her tightly while she came down.

"Thank you, Master."

"Unless we are in public scene or I direct you otherwise, you'll still call me Grayson."

"Grayson." She hummed dreamily.

He helped her to stand and directed her to the bed. Her legs were barely able to keep her upright.

"Lay down on your stomach." While she settled herself, he retrieved his toy bag and pulled out the Aloe ointment he used for aftercare.

"What's that?"

"It'll sooth the ache. I'm afraid you've pinked up well. It may be a little difficult to sit down tomorrow." He pulled out a bottle of paracetamol from his bag also. "Here take this as well. It will help you sleep. It can be uncomfortable the first time. You're not used to it." He rubbed the ointment in with tender care

"I'm sure people would say I'm mad. I enjoyed you spanking me so much that I need to take painkillers to sleep."

"But the point is you enjoyed it, and I'm taking care of you. I don't hide what I am, Sophie. If people ask about my sexual orientation, I will admit I'm a full-time Dom. I'm the owner of a club. There are always people who call me filthy for what I like. I'm not a masochist for pain. There are certain limits we need to talk about. We cannot go into this blindly if it is what you choose. There may be things I want to do to you that you don't want."

"Fisting; Anal or vaginal. I don't like the sound of that." She interrupted him with a screwed up facial expression. It was so cute he couldn't help but laugh. He helped her to sit up on a cushion. He handed her one of the warmed up goat's milk pancakes. A staple in life.

"Eat." She took it and ate. "That is something I have experimented with before. I can see that it brings some women great pleasure. At the moment though, it is not something I would even consider doing with you. You're too tight. And an anal virgin?" The last part was a question.

"I asked my boyfriend to try it, but it didn't work. He used his finger, but his cock was too painful. Maybe I should add no anal to those limits as well. This feels weird talking to you about this stuff. My mind is saying I should be embarrassed, but I'm not."

"I'm glad you don't feel ashamed talking of these things. It's a good start. As for the anal. Would you allow me to try? I suspect that your boyfriend was not aware of how to prepare you for that type of sex."

She bit her lip as she thought. It did nothing for the erection he still had.

"Ok, but if I don't like it, we add it to the no list."

"Of course. I'm not into blade or fire play. I would like to use whips and floggers on you. How do you feel about that?"

"I'm glad about the blade and fire play. Nervous of the whips and floggers but willing to try."

She finished her pancake and reached out to take another one. He could see the moment it suddenly dawned on her and how she withdrew her hand before it touched the food.

"May I have another please?"

He smiled.

"In a minute. I'm not going to be able to concentrate on anything until I get rid of this." He pointed at his groin. "I want you to ride me."

He stroked himself a few times while Sophie moved the tray to the floor. She straddled him.

"Condom?" He whispered into her ear.

"I'm clean and on the pill."

"I was checked after I fired my last PA."

"Please let me have you in me bare."

His answer came in the form of pulling her down on his cock. Relief, he was sheathed within her tight pussy. It was home. She clenched down on him, and he helped her to start moving up and down his length. Every time she swallowed him whole, it must have been banging her sore backside down on his legs. She proved to be the kinky little girl who he thought she was when she brought herself down faster and further. They were in a steady rhythm now. He was lost in her eyes; they were joined as one. His perfect woman. His. She was his. And as he emptied his seed into her warm havens, he knew he'd fight tooth and nail to keep her.

"Yes."

She uttered breathlessly, drawing him from his post orgasmic haze.

"Sorry?"

"I'm yours. Twenty-four-seven. I am everything that you need, because I'm already half in love with you."

"I think I'm already fully in love with you." Was his breathless reply.

ONE YEAR LATER

I now pronounce you Mr & Mrs Grayson Moore. You may kiss the Bride.

Er...Mr Moore I think maybe you should remove your hand from under Mrs Moore's dress and your tongue from her throat. I do believe there are lots of guests watching.

CHAPTER SEVEN

Sally-Bridgewater

Three Years Later

At least the plane journey had been in first class. It seemed to take forever to fly to Phoenix from the UK. Sally had never been one for travelling. Shame it was part of her job, an intrepid investigative journalist for the London Daily Magazine. It might sound like a cheap little rag, and well, to be honest, before she arrived, it had been. She got the big stories that helped it grow. Many of them were thanks to her kind benefactor. But enough of him for now. He finally gave her the go-ahead to go after Grayson Moore, and she was going to do everything within her power to destroy the arrogant movie star once and for all. He deserved no kindness from her, and he wouldn't get it. He would be penniless and alone in the gutter when she was done with him. That was how much venom she felt towards him.

The car pulled up to the run down shack of a house in the middle of the red sandstone desert. So this was where the poor little Indian boy, who made good, originated. She wondered if they would let him back into his homelands after she had finished destroying him. Judging by the emails that had led her to this place. She very much doubted that and, boy, did that feel so perfect.

A raven hair woman opened the door to the house. Sally got out of the car, grabbed her bag, which contained her laptop, recorder, and notebook and went to greet her.

"Hello. Swan, isn't it?"

"Yes, Miss Bridgewater." They shook hands. Grayson Moore's sister was tiny. She couldn't have been more than five foot three, if that. Sally knew that Grayson's mother was white and only his father was Native American. But Swan, as she was called in her mother tongue, looked pure Indian.

"Please call me Sally." She responded politely.

"Sally, come in."

She followed the young girl into the house. It was little more than a kitchen and seating area with room to the side that held mattresses on the floor for beds. It was spotlessly clean though.

"I'm sorry. My home is basic. I'd rather die than accept any of my brother's money."

"I understand." Sally motioned to a chair. "Shall we sit, and you can tell me more?"

"I'll get you a drink first. You must have had a long trip. I've never been out of Navajo lands. I choose not to, because I don't like the world I've seen in print and on the TV beyond our borders. But I know how long it takes to travel anywhere, and I looked on a map, and London is so far away."

Sally tried not to roll her eyes. This girl was going to be easy to manipulate. She was a complete simpleton.

"It has taken me almost twenty-four hours to travel here."

"That is a long time." Swan handed her a drink. It was a putrid green in colour.

"What is this?" She inquired with genuine interest.

"It's cactus juice. I make it myself."

"I can't say I've had that before. Thank you." She took a sip. It was the most disgusting thing she'd ever had in her mouth, and she'd had some pretty revolting things in there to facilitate a story. She tried not to pull a face.

"It's delicious." She placed the glass down on the table. "You don't mind if I record everything that we talk about, do you? It just makes it easier, and I write everything up later."

"Of course not. There's nothing I'll tell you that I'm ashamed of. My brother is a disgrace to his ancestry."

This naïve girl was going to be perfect for her plans.

"I know little about him." The massive lie quickly left Sally's lips, "but what I do know makes me sick." She turned on her recorder.

"That is the horrible part. He was such a lovely child. So caring as a brother. Willing to do anything for me. Prominent in the community as a whole. He volunteered whenever it was needed. Then he got that job offer. He changed overnight." Swan rested her elbows on the table to help aid her thinking process it seemed.

"The part in the first Renegade movie?"

"Yes. We didn't even know that he auditioned. He told us that he was going away with a couple of his friends for a week. When he came back, he said he was going to be a movie star. Mom and Dad were happy for him, but I was sceptical. He's a more sensitive soul than an action movie star. I've seen some of those films. All they do is run around and kill people. Rescue the girl. That sort of thing. Where is the side of Grayson that I know? Or knew." Swan spat out bitterly.

The Indian had finished her cactus juice and was pouring some more. The bottle was held out to Sally.

"I'm fine thank you." Sally took another sip of the juice to look polite. She hoped that it wouldn't make her sick later. "Have you watched his films?"

"I watched the first one. Mom and Dad had a massive party for the premiere of it. Every time he was on the screen people were applauding. I didn't enjoy it though. Too much of my brother on display. And that scene at the end, when he rescues the woman and they fornicate on the beach, it's disgusting. The way he tells her what she can and can't do. That isn't romantic." Swan shook her head in disgust.

"Critics have applauded that scene, saying it is good to see an action hero with a bite finally." Sally happened to enjoy it as well. Despite hating Grayson, she had to admit he had a pretty perfect body, made for the big screen.

"The critics know nothing." The young girl's face turned red with anger, "That film made a mockery of my ancestry. They purposely chose Grayson because he is half Native American. They are vile creatures who drew him into their web of lies and deceit. Manipulated him into someone, no something, I no longer recognise. And he allowed it to happen."

"How did he change?"

"Sexually."

"What do you mean?" Sally asked.

"He was virgin when he left here. My mother brought us up to be good people. To save our purity for when we are married. But they turned him into the wrong sort of man."

"What do you mean by the wrong sort of man?" They were getting to the good stuff now. That bit that could destroy Grayson's reputation; he was known as a womaniser, and people didn't care because he appeared to be a nice person.

"The kind of man who turns his back on his ancestry just so that he can get sex."

"Turn his back?" Sally was almost rubbing her hands in glee, an evil cackle stuck in the back of her throat desperately screaming for release.

"Yes. You've seen the reports. He always has a different woman on his arm, sometimes more than one. His ex-PA said he would pay them to have sex with him. He gave away his money to sluts so that he could get his kicks when we, his family lived in poverty."

"I thought you said that you wouldn't take a penny from him?" She needed to make sure the story was cast iron tight so that Grayson's solicitors could do nothing to stop it reaching worldwide.

"I don't want a penny." Swan snapped back. "I like my home. We're a big community though. People are suffering here. Individuals on whom he could have spent that money. We need a new town centre hall; the old one is damaged and may not last long. The Chiefs need respect; they cannot have it when that is their base." Swan shifted in her chair when she spoke

"Has Grayson been asked to donate?"

"He shouldn't need to be asked. He turned his back on his family. He knows nothing about what is happening here anymore. He should still keep in touch with us and aim to help. Do you know that last time he came back here?" Swan's voice was raised in great fury.

"No."

"Two year's ago. He brought his slut of a wife here. The two of them dripping in gold and designer clothes. Her with a dog collar around her neck. It's disgusting watching them together. She walks behind him, only speaks when he allows her to. She isn't allowed to eat anything that he doesn't let her or feed her himself. It's sick. Grayson Moore is not the great film star he makes himself out to be. He is a traitor to his blood. He neglects his family and treats his wife like a pet." Swan lowered her head towards the Dictaphone as she spoke. Each word was coming out with such revulsion and vehemence.

"As well as the money he's spent on the woman of ill repute; where else do you think he's neglected the community." It was time to go in for the killer blows.

"Those clubs he bought." Bingo! She had Grayson's career in the palm of her hand and was about to squash him like the bug he was.

"You mean..." She lowered her voice so it looked like she was repulsed as well. "The clubs that he bought?"

"Yes. Those clubs. He would rather buy a sex club than help out his family." Swan's rage was so potent that it bubbled over in a display of aggression that saw her pick her cup up and throw it at the wall. The green slime slid down the wall and mixed with the sandy dust that appeared to be a feature in the house and everywhere else in this barren place.

Swan's hatred of her brother was pure gold. Sally was finding it so hard not to jump up and hug the girl. This would be her finest article yet.

"I'm sorry." Swan got to her feet and grabbed a cloth.

"It's alright." Sally took the cloth from her and made a show of wiping up the cactus juice. "After hearing everything you have to say, I'm as angry as you are. He can't be allowed to get away with this."

"You're going to destroy him?" Swan looked at her hopefully.

"It seems to me as though he wants to forget who he is. I'm not going to allow that to happen. Mr Moore has ignored his roots for far too long now. It's time that he was reminded of his upbringing and the family that gave him the skills he needs to be who he is today." Sally came back over to Swan and pulled the now crying girl into her arms. "Yes, Swan. I'm going to demolish your brother's life as he knows it."

CHAPTER EIGHT

Grayson

"It's beautiful." Grayson watched Sophie wipe away a tear. She was lounging on a plush leather sofa in their LA home, reading the script he had written with his screen-writer friend. It was five years in the making, but they finally finished it.

"Really?"

"Yes. The way you work your ancestry into the story is incredible. I can really feel your heart in it." She giggled. "The Academy really needs to get this on the Oscar nominations."

"I'm not sure it's that good, but I'm happy to settle for critical acclaim and maybe the highest grossing film of all time. It's about time Avatar stood down from that."

Sophie took the script and whacked him gently with it. His heart leapt. Even after four years together she knew how to get him going.

"I think someone is looking to be a naughty little imp doing that to her Master."

"I...er..." She licked her lips.

"On your knees before me." His wife quickly obeyed and settled between his open thighs. Her long brown hair cascaded over her shoulders like a waterfall over a rocky cliff. "You know what happens when you sass me."

"I have to apologise."

"You do. And how do you apologise to me."

"By sucking your cock till it explodes down my throat." Fuck! The words out of her mouth were like the most beautiful symphony. Grayson made quick work of freeing himself from his jeans. He stroked his length up and down while Sophie sat back on her heels and waited for him to allow her to begin her part in this.

"You want my cock little one?"

"Yes, please." Her words were breathless.

"How much do you want it?"

"I'm desperate for it. To taste your desire, to choke on your size."

He moaned his response.

"Lick me from the base to tip." He sat back to watch.

Sophie poked her tongue out from between her ruby red lips and brought it down on his length. He gripped the chair as she repeated the movement.

"Sod going slow." He took the back of her head and thrust it down on his length. She gagged at the surprise; recovered and swallowed him into the back of her throat. He was controlling the movement now. Using her mouth to get himself off. They both liked it this way, because it was the trust that she had given to him. His hands twirled tighter in her hair pulling on her scalp.

"Damn baby, that feels so good. You really are good at apologising to me. I think I like you being a naughty little girl."

Sophie purred in the back of her throat at the praise. It sent tremors right down his dick. He was going to come. Grayson pushed her head back down his length one final time and held it there as he emptied himself into his wife's mouth. She took everything he had. He was spent and released Sophie and collapse back onto his chair.

"Clean me up." He still had a little bit of dominating tone in his voice, although most of it was covered by contentment. Sophie licked him clean and then popped him back in his trousers. She went back onto her knees in front of him.

"Into my lap little one." Like a puppy who being praised, she wiggled her backside and scrambled up into his arms. He stroked the collar around her neck. It was a simple necklace made of gold with a diamond encrusted 'G' and 'S' woven together as a pendant.

"I love you, Master."

"I love you too." He smiled. "I think after that you've earned some play time. Do you want to go to the club later?" The club had been one of his first purchases when he had enough money to buy it. He'd been taken to it when he first entered the world of showbiz. The Fifty Shades of Grey film was popular, and an unscrupulous pimp decided to jump on the bandwagon of the Dominant and Submissive lifestyle. Shame the services he offered were from women who had been sold into slavery to pay off debts. He'd been so disgusted that the second he had the money he bought the club and shut it down. He helped the women find new lives away from the pain and fear they had been living under. What shocked him more was that several had become so ingrained in the lifestyle that they didn't want to leave it. That was when he decided to turn the club into a proper BDSM one. Membership, health checks, pension plans, the works. The girls were employed to waitress and scene with the club's highly trained masters, if they wanted to. Several told him he saved their lives. They no longer feared what would happen to them. They enjoyed sex once more. He couldn't have been prouder of his decision.

Sophie bounced on his lap, and it brought him back to the here and now. "Can we please? You promised me a violet wand the next time we went. Please." She was giving him the puppy dog eyes, which meant he could deny her nothing.

"If you can be a good girl for the rest of the day, we can. Go do your PA work."

"Thank you." Sophie got off his lap and went off to their home office. Grayson got to his feet and went into the kitchen. He needed a cold drink after that climax. His legs were still a little wobbly. He grabbed a Coke from the fridge and picked up his phone that had been charging on the counter. Thirty-eight missed calls? Several texts and voicemails. He'd put it on silent when they'd been reading the script, as he didn't want anything to disturb Sophie's concentration as she finished the last act. He'd even turned off the house phone. Grayson used his touch identification to open his notifications. They were from his agent and several other identified sources. There were some from James and Matthew as well. What the hell was going on? He pressed the call button to his agent, but before there was an answer, an ear-piercing scream came from Sophie. He dropped his phone and found himself running through the house to the office.

"Sophie." He slammed the door open to find her crying at her desk. "What's happened?"

She pointed at the screen of her computer. His mouth fell opened as he read.

Multi-millionaire movie star, Grayson Moore, leaves his ancestry behind to run a string of sex clubs.

What the fuck was going on? He read on.

Grayson Moore, the star of the Renegade films has left the Chiefs of his tribe to fend for themselves in squalor while he purchased, Infinity, a club that has been involved in sex slavery. The twenty-eight-year-old movie star even takes his wife to these clubs and leads her around on a dog collar. Sophie Moore, nee North, is the sister of British billionaire James North who is also well known for his warped views of women. Moore's sister, Swan, lives in a one-bedroom hut in the Navajo Desert, stated that she was appalled at her brother's behaviour. She called him a disgrace to his Native American ancestry. Swan feels that he was corrupted by the glittering lights of Hollywood and that there is nothing of the caring brother left. He hasn't even visited his family in two years."

That was enough; he couldn't read anymore. Grayson picked the computer up off the desk and threw it hard at the wall. Sophie screamed again.

"Grayson." She called out in fear. It permeated his brain,

which was filled with anger and fury.

"My fucking sister. That's the biggest pile of crap I've ever read."

"I know. We need to get onto your agent?"

He picked up the phone and dialled.

"Grayson. Thank God. Have you seen the news?" His agent sounded harassed when he answered the phone.

"Just. What the fuck is going on?" Grayson placed the phone on speaker so that Sophie could hear everything that was being said.

"Sally Bridgewater of the London Daily apparently did an interview with your sister. I've no idea how she got access to her. We've always kept her out of the press for this reason exactly."

"Sally Bridgewater?" Sophie exclaimed. "She's been after my brother and his friends. She's playing a game with us."

"Can we get the story dismissed as a bunch of lies?" Grayson added.

"You're not going to like what I'm about to say but no. Everything she had printed is accurate as far as we can tell." His agent replied.

"Accurate." He yelled into the phone. "The article accuses me of neglecting the Chiefs of my tribe. I've given loads of money to them; four years ago, I gave them half a million to build a new community centre."

"Um." His agent hesitated on the other end of the phone.

"What?"

"Maybe Mrs North should leave the room."

"Sophie and I have no secrets."

"You gave the money to your last PA for the community centre. The audit trail shows it never got there. It went straight to the women who were employed to bed you." His agent went quiet.

Sophie turned away from Grayson's touch, a loud sob ripping from her throat.

"I've been a complete idiot."

"I think we all have been. I've got the solicitors working

on what we can do and say now. I'll call you back later. Stay home. Don't go out. Make sure Sophie stays home as well. The article talks a lot about your lifestyle and not in a good way."

"Ok." It was all he could say before he hung up and replaced the phone. "Soph?"

She came into his arms with genuine love in her eyes.

"I'm scared." She whispered into his chest.

"I know. We've got a good team around us now. We'll let them sort it. We know the truth. That is all that matters."

"You should phone your parents. Warn them what is happening. They'll probably have more press arriving to ask questions."

"I'll get one of the guards to bring them here for safety."

"For Swan's safety as well, I think your dad will go mad when he finds out."

"She's created her own problems. I'm not going to waste any time on her." His sister could go to hell, as far as he was concerned. Alright, he hadn't been back to his Navajo lands in two years, but his parents and friends had visited them loads. He'd even hosted some of the Chiefs. He picked up the phone to call his parents, but it rang in his hands. The caller ID showed it was the club manager, his good friend Wolf.

"Wolf?"

"Hi mate. I know you're probably busy with the fallout of the article, but we've got a bit of a situation down at the club?"

"What is it?"

"A riot."

"A riot." Sophie gasped.

"Hawk, the club. They set fire to it. We managed to get the girls who live there out, but a couple got hurt in the process.

"I'm on my way." He threw the phone back in the holder.

"We were told not to go out." Sophie grabbed his hand.

"You stay here. I'll get a guard to sit with you."

"No." She urged.

"I have to see and help the girls."

"Then I'm going with you." Sophie was defiant.

"It's too dangerous."

"The girls will be distressed. They know me." She was right about that one. Some of the girls had been through so many horrors. He and his wife looked after them and gave them a home and a life.

"You stay with me at all times."

"Yes, Master."

He touched the collar at her neck again.

"You are a good man Grayson. Don't listen to words in the article."

"As long as I have you by my side and you believe in me, I won't."

"You've got me always. Till death do us part, remember." Sophie replied.

The closer to the club they got, the busier the streets LA streets became. Grayson had clubs in LA, London, Las Vegas, and Florida. He was a silent partner, up until now. All the clubs were used to hurt and degrade women in the past all in the name of so-called BDSM. He turned them around to be places where people could happily live the lifestyle without fear or punishment that they didn't want. None of that was talked about in the article.

He turned his car onto the road where the club was. The red and blue lights of the troopers, ambulances, and fire engines flashed. Shit. He wondered how severe was this fire? The answer was given to him straight away when the burnt out remnants of a building loomed in front of him. Sophie gasped beside him and grabbed his hand.

Wolf ran up to greet them as Grayson showed his ID through the window of the car to pass through the police cordon.

"I'm sorry, but I thought I had to call you."

"It's ok, where are the girls?" Grayson jumped out the car and went around to Sophie's side to help her out. He kept a tight hold of her hand. The car that contained his bodyguards stopped behind him, and the two burly men filed out to stand beside him and Sophie.

"Jane and Callie are in the hospital. Smoke inhalation and minor burns. They were sleeping upstairs and had to be rescued by the firemen. Alexia is with Gina and Becky in the cafe. She was visiting for Jane's training."

"Burns." Sophie squeezed his hand. It was the only word that he'd heard as well.

"Wolf, will you take Sophie into the café? Carl, go with them." One of the bodyguards nodded. "I'm going to talk to police." He could feel Sophie tense beside him. He pulled her aside.

"It's ok. I'll be just over there. You know Wolf and Carl. They'll protect you."

"Ok."

"Good girl. I love you."

"I know. I love you too."

He reluctantly let go of Sophie's hand, but he knew she would be safer in the café than out here in the open. He could already see the crowds of onlookers that had formed. The flashes of cameras from reporters dying to get the best picture of the unfolding situation. The high from his earlier climax was well and truly gone.

He strode over to the police officer who appeared to be in charge, but before he could get there, a commotion appeared in front of him. A large crowd of people were after him. Waving banners in his direction and shouting insults. The guard with him grabbed him and tried to pull him away, but it was too late. The crowd surrounded him. Flashes of cameras blinded him.

"Pervert!" A woman slapped him hard on the face.

"Sicko." Another kicked out at him. His bodyguard tried to get in front of him.

"Mr Moore, do you have any answers to the fact you've

neglected your family so you can have sex with whores?" A reporter thrust a microphone into his face.

"Is there to be an investigation into the women who work at the club. Have you been involved in human trafficking?"

Grayson stared at the reporter who had posed that question. Where had that one come from? He was involved in nothing of the sort. Everything seemed like it was happening in slow motion. The world that he knew was falling apart, and he felt like he was standing there just watching it.

"Grayson." Sophie's cries echoed out above the crowd. She was nearby and not in the café. He looked around to see her fighting her way through the crowd. The other bodyguard, Carl and Wolf with her. She reached him the same time as the police started to push the crowd away. He grabbed her and pulled her to him.

"Move," Carl shouted at him. He nodded and started running for his car. He had Sophie's hand and was pulling her with him. The crowd followed still shouting the insults. "Faster." The bodyguard was pushing them along now. Sophie's hand slipped from his, and she fell. He tried to turn back to get to her, but Carl pulled him away. The crowd surrounded her. He couldn't see what was happening. Grayson punched Carl square on the jaw, and he was free. He went back to Sophie, pushing people away from her. The police did the same and formed a cordon around them. He pulled her into his arms, checking every inch of her for signs that she was hurt. Her hands and knees were scrapped. He would clean them up later. He got to her neck. Her collar, it was gone. Sophie let out a pained cry and opened her hands. In them was her collar...broken.

CHAPTER NINE

Sophie

Sophie turned in the bed to face Grayson. He'd finally fallen asleep an hour ago. It was the early hours of the morning; mind you, she wasn't really sure what time it was as they were somewhere over the Atlantic on their way to England. After the incident earlier that day, her brother phoned and insisted that Grayson bring Sophie to England for protection. Neither of them had had the strength to argue. Grayson's face was covered in lines of stress even in his sleep. He had a black eye forming where he was hit by one of the protestors. Sophie touched her neck. Her collar was gone, ripped from her body by the crowd who proclaimed her free of the monster. Its remnants lay in a box in her suitcase. Grayson assured her that as soon as they got to England, he would look for someone to fix it for her. It wouldn't ever be the same though. It was tainted now.

The plane hit a bit of turbulence; it did little to settle her stomach. Maybe a glass of water would help. Throwing her legs out of bed, she grabbed a robe and tied it around her waist. Carl and Damian, their bodyguards, were sleeping in their seats when she stepped into the galley kitchen to find a bottle of water. The stewardess jumped to her feet.

"Mrs Moore what can I get for you?"

"It's alright. I just want a bottle of water."

The stewardess was at her side and pulled out two bottles before she had a chance to think.

"Still or sparkling."

"Sparkling please."

"Is there anything else you want?"

Sophie ran her fingers through her hair.

"The ability to sleep."

"I wish I could pull that out of the cupboard for you."
The stewardess smiled sympathetically. "Mr Moore is a
good man no matter what they say. And I can see that you
really love him. That's what counts."

"Thank you. That means a lot."

"Goodnight, Mrs Moore."

Sophie nodded her reply and pushed the door to the
bedroom open. Grayson was sitting up on the bed rubbing
his eyes.

"What's wrong?" He queried.

"I needed a drink."

"Damn, I'm sorry. I didn't get you one before we settled
down."

"That's ok." She reassured. "You had a lot on your
mind."

"No, it's not." He snapped at her. "I'm supposed to be
looking after you."

"Hey." She climbed into the bed and rested her hand on
his strong jawline. "You are looking after me. Don't doubt
that because of what is happening."

"I let your hand go." He looked so sad.

"You were being pushed along by Carl and Damian. I had
high heels on. It was a dangerous situation. It was going to
happen, and there was nothing we could do to stop it. I'm
just glad they got you to safety before anything worse happened." She gave him a kiss to show she was not upset
about what had happened.

"Worse, they broke your collar."

"Which can be fixed." She'd been distraught about the
collar. She loved having the symbol of being owned and
cared for, but there was something that she was more worried about. "When I saw the crowd around you I was so
scared. I knew you told me to stay with Wolf and Carl, but I
couldn't. I had visions of them beating you like my brother.
All I could think about was getting to you and protecting
you from that."

"You were terrified that what happened to James might

happen to me?"

"Yes. When that woman hit you, I wanted to rip her hand off." She quieted; the thoughts she had in her head were all jumbled up. She needed to collate them before she spoke. "I love our life, and I don't want anything to change."

He pulled her close to him.

"You're not scared of physical violence to me, it's the emotional scars it will leave." He understood her perfectly.

"Yes. I'm scared that you'll become like James and stop being who you are. You've done nothing wrong, yet you are being reviled because of it."

"I'm not James; the situation is different. I was scared out there today. I will admit that. But not because of who I am. As you say, I've done nothing wrong, and I'm not going to change. You misbehave little one, and I'm going to pink that backside of yours until it glows. What upset me most is that the reports criticise me for neglecting my roots. I need to reflect and reconcile myself with that. Maybe I have done my ancestry wrong. They never got the money for the community centre; I didn't follow it up."

She had to interrupt him there. "You can't be held responsible for that. You gave the money to your PA in good faith to help out the Chiefs. You were not to know he paid women instead."

"But I should have checked." She could see that there was no point in discussing this further. Grayson had made his mind up that the blame lay partly with him. He would see it right though. That was the sort of man that he was.

"We can think more on it tomorrow. I think we should get some sleep."

"Sleep in my arms?" He asked.

"Of course." She would never deny him.

The plane landed four hours later, and they were whisked away to James' country mansion in Yorkshire where she crawled into bed for almost fourteen hours of sleep. Sophie felt awful. Lack of sleep and tears had left her with puffy eyes. She had scrapes on her hands and knees, and every time she tried to eat something, she felt sick. Grayson made her eat, of course. He seemed more relaxed this morning and focused. They were both in the kitchen with a lavish spread of breakfast laid before them. Grayson was on the phone to Wolf for an update on Jane's and Callie's conditions when James popped his head around the door.

"I hear someone needs a cuddle from her big brother." Emotion hit her, and she burst into tears.

"James, you're not supposed to make her cry." Amy pushed her husband out of the way and came to give Sophie a hug. Grayson held his finger up to show he would be a couple of minutes and left the room to finish his call.

"Sorry, Sis." Her brother wiped away her tears.

"It's alright. I'm a little emotional."

"I think you'll find that James thinks all women are emotional." Amy patted her stomach. She was five months pregnant with their second child.

"Where's Thomas?" Sophie asked

"With mum and dad. They wanted to spoil him before his little sister arrives and takes all the attention." James poured himself a coffee. "Where is Mrs Aimes?" Mrs Aimes was the housekeeper of James' country home. She and her family ran and lived in the house even when the North family wasn't there.

"She and Mr Aimes have gone to town. They needed more supplies for dinner."

"I hope she is cooking her beef dish with the pepper sauce." Sonia came into the kitchen with an even bigger belly. She was six months pregnant, Matthew, her partner and James' bodyguard, entered behind with the suitcases. "I'm so hungry and craving red meat all the time."

"I got some red meat you can have it you want it, my little dove." Matthew Carter joked with Sonia.

"Oh, I'm craving that as well."

"Oh thank God I'm not the only one." James' PA, Marie, appeared as well. Sonia was starting to wonder how many people had travelled here.

"Please don't tell me you want it again. I must be getting old, but I don't think I've recovered from twice on the plane yet." Callum, her husband and finance director of North Enterprises, poured a coffee when he walked in before collapsing on a chair.

"Welcome to the world of pregnant women you two. It will slow down soon when they can't see their toes and have to be hoisted off the sofa." James laughed and took a seat next to her at the table.

"Slow down, she's only four months. I still got five to go!" Callum replied.

"Hi, Marie, Callum, Sonia, Matthew. Is there anyone else coming?" Sophie was a little in shock at the sudden invasion.

"Just us," Amy replied and sat next to her husband.

"When we heard what was happening we all had to come and support you. That woman is a nuisance." Marie took a croissant from the pile on the table. "I hope that you are going to cut her off this time, Matthew."

"Believe me," Sonia answered before Matthew could. "If I get my hands on her, she won't be writing any more stories anytime soon."

"Ladies, let the gentlemen deal with Sally Bridgewater. You three concentrate on the babies inside you." If looks could kill, Matthew Carter would be flayed alive.

"It's alright. Grayson has his lawyers on the case. We just need to prove that he helped out the girls in the club not force them into anything. They are also trying to show he had the intention to fix the community centre."

"What about all the lies concerning your relationship with him?" Amy questioned.

"We had a chat about that on the plane. We know the truth, and that is we're in love. That is all that matters." Sophie smiled at that thought. Her first smile since the article had been published.

"Oh. I think I'm going to cry." Sonia snuffled. Matthew

handed her a tissue.

"Another thing you've got to come to Callum."

"Already there mate." The accountant handed Marie a tissue from his pocket; she also had tears streaming down her cheeks.

"Woah." Grayson stepped back in the room. "We having a party?"

The men all stood and shook hands.

"Not a party. Not yet anyway." James folded his arms across his broad chest. "Someone has tried to mess with my sister's life. The same person who has messed with all our lives recently. Enough is enough. Tomorrow, the girls go for a ladies' day, no arguments about that from any of you when three of you are pregnant." Amy went to open her mouth but shut it straight away again. "We are going to figure out how to bring Sally Bridgewater down once and for all."

CHAPTER TEN

Grayson

"Mr Smith will see you now gentlemen." Along with James, Matthew and Callum, Grayson stood and followed the secretary into the opulent boardroom. It was decorated with the finest wooden furniture. The glass panels of the windows had excellent views over the whole of London; no wonder there was a restaurant on the roof that offered afternoon tea with Champagne at a hundred pounds a time.

A portly gentleman sat at the head of the boardroom table. He stood when they entered.

"Mr Moore I expected a visit from you when I heard that you were in the UK but not Mr North and friends as well. I hope I don't need security." It was time to rub the smug smile of the editor in chief of London Daily. James stepped forward.

"I think you'll find that I'll be the one calling security or just having Mr Carter here remove you from the premises." Mr Smith's smile faded especially when he looked up at Matthew who cracked his knuckles.

"You can't do that." Mr Smith tried to be stern, but the underlying fear in his voice showed. Grayson was pretty sure that the man was about to piss himself.

"I think you'll find I can. You see, at eight am this morning, I became the owner of London Daily." James stood back with a smug smile on his face. "It was a brilliant idea of my Finance Director actually. He's been on me to diversify for a while now. And when an opportunity presented itself, I had to take it."

"You can't just walk in here and spout lies like that." Mr Smith banged his fist on the desk.

"Matthew," James called his bodyguard forward. Matthew pulled a document, which Grayson knew to be the contract for the sale, from inside his jacket and thrust it at Mr Smith with a grunt before stepping back.

"I'll think you'll find that everything is in order. In future, I would appreciate it if you speak to me with respect I demand as your boss." Mr Smith picked up the paper and turned white as a sheet when he read it. Grayson smirked, and James winked at him.

"What do you want?" The editor's demeanour had slumped, and he fell back into his chair. James' reputation for sharp business acumen was well known.

"The first task Callum undertook for me was to bring up all the personal files of the company. There will be lots of changes there, but I have one pressing one. I'm sure you can guess what?"

"Sally Bridgewater."

"Exactly." James reply was laced with menace. "Callum, would you care to explain?"

"My pleasure." Callum stepped forward and placed a briefcase on the table. He opened it and pulled out a file before putting it in front of Mr Smith. Grayson watched everything with glee, because he knew what was coming next.

"This is the file of complaints against Miss Bridgewater." The file had to be at least an inch thick. Some of which were still not settled. Callum opened the file and put five pieces of paper on the table. "These are currently in court, and our solicitor is not confident of a settlement in favour of Miss Bridgewater. Also, as I understand it, Mr Moore here will be releasing a statement later today to repute Miss Bridgewater's allegations in the latest article that the magazine published. He will also be issuing his intention to sue the magazine and Miss Bridgewater for defamation."

Mr Smith looked towards Grayson. His response was to scowl; this was the man who gave that bitch the go ahead to publish that article. Callum pulled another piece of paper from his briefcase.

"This is my calculation of the cost to the company now owned by Mr North. I'm sure you will agree that doesn't make good reading."

"It certainly doesn't" James interjected. "And I'm not about to suffer those losses. The way Callum tells me we have two alternatives. Firstly, liquidate the company making everyone redundant to pay the legal costs. Of course, top management, like yourself would suffer greatly from this alternative. Editor in Chief of an international magazine and it went under during your time in charge. I'm sure that would make it hard to get any future jobs." James paused there for dramatic effect. "Or we could get rid of the culprit. Show that we do not support her. Issue apologies for articles and offer cursory damages to those involved. What alternative do you suggest Mr Smith?"

"It will not be legal. She's done nothing wrong."

"These court cases prove that is not true." James pressed his finger down onto the documents that Callum had laid out. Mr Smith looked between them all.

"I'll call her in immediately. She'll be gone by lunchtime."

Grayson let out a long breath. Retribution was his.

CHAPTER ELEVEN

Sophie

"I think I'm actually bored of being pampered." Amy stretched out a long limb and wiggled her toes to check the turquoise coloured varnish that was just painted on. Sophie leant forward to admire it also.

"I know the feeling." Sonia moaned from under a face mask. "Matthew won't even let me go to the gun range anymore. Apparently, the noise is too loud for his son's delicate growing ears. I did tell him that it would be nothing but a mute pop to the baby." Sonia told Sophie the night before that after weeks of arguing over finding out the sex of their baby they'd made the decision, and it was a boy. Sonia laughed when telling her and had even did a display of a strutting peacock. Apparently, Matthew walked around that way for days afterwards.

"Callum and I have no hope of peace and quiet. Owen thinks he is a lion, at the moment, and spends most of the day roaring." Marie added. Owen was Marie's and Callum's adopted son. He was Marie's sister's boy, but unfortunately, her sister died under horrific circumstances when she gave birth.

"This is why Grayson and I don't want children yet," Sophie added with mocking supremacy.

"You'll have to have a baby soon, or your mum and dad will expect me to keep having more to make up the numbers. They want lots of grandchildren." Amy shifted from her seating position. "I've got enough stretch marks to last me a lifetime."

"And my brother worships every one of them. You keep pushing them out for the North repopulation team." Sophie was laughing this time; Marie and Sonia joined in. The pampering was indeed becoming tedious. They could only sit around and drink tea for so long when worried about what their husbands or partners were up to.

"You know what? Let's go to Betty's in York. I haven't been there for ages. I want afternoon tea and fat rascals." Sophie stood up.

"Custard tarts." Sonia joined her.

"One question first." Marie held her hand up, "What is a fat rascal?"

"A scone made with lard, fruit, sugar...everything that is not good for you really," Sophie answered.

"I'm in." Marie picked her bag up. "Amy?"

"I don't know. James said we should stay here." Sophie could see the reticence on her blonde sister-in-law's face.

"Carl and Damian are here. I'll make sure they come with us. But we have the best bodyguard in Sonia with us anyway." Marie replied, and Sonia smirked proudly.

"You know James is going to spank me for doing this."

"I'm hoping Grayson does the same." Sophie chuckled.

Sonia let out a lascivious moan.

"Oh God. You've got her dreaming about the whipping she will get now." Marie laughed.

"Let's go and be naughty little Subbies before our Dom's realise." And with that final word from Amy, they were all out the door.

Carl and Damian moaned most of the journey to York, but as they all walked through the streets of York towards Betty's, they settled down and relaxed. There had been a phone call to one of the bodyguard's mobiles when they'd left the house. They all knew it was James or Matthew, as they were the ones who had their significant others 'chipped'. The phone was passed to Sonia who informed the person on the other end of the line that pregnant women needed cakes and afternoon tea. They surmised it was Matthew when she told the caller they had bodyguards, and she was deadly, as only he well knew, and that they would be perfectly safe. They would go for tea and come straight back. She confirmed that she would accept her punishment later and looked forward to receiving it, before hanging up and throwing the phone towards Damian. When it rang again a few seconds later, she glared at him until he put it back in his pocket and turned the music up so it couldn't be heard.

"Please, can we go in here?" Sonia clapped her hands while looking hopefully at a shop. Sophie looked up at the sign above her. The Armoury. Of course, of all the places that the bodyguard wanted to visit, it would have to be this one. Sophie herself looked lovingly at the cocktail bar across the road, but she knew with three pregnant women that was never going to happen. "I really want to get Drew a present."

"Drew?" Amy asked.

"The baby. Matthew and I decided on the name last night. Andrew James Carter. Already shortened to Drew."

"Oh, I love it," Amy exclaimed, and they all hugged in the middle of the street. "James is going to be so proud." Her sister-in-law wiped away a tear.

"Enough sappiness. Let's go look at knives for a baby." Marie raised an eyebrow. "I can't believe I just said that."

"Surreal isn't it." Sonia laughed, and despite being six months pregnant skipped into the shop.

When Sophie entered, Sonia already had several knives out and was looking at them. Marie went over to assist. Amy threaded her arm through Sophie's and pulled her aside.

"How are you feeling?" Amy asked.

"I'm ok." She replied.

"And now tell me the real answer."

"Honestly, I'm just tired. Jet lag. I know whatever the guys are doing will make everything alright. I'm just hoping it isn't murder." Sophie rubbed at the wedding ring on her finger while she spoke. She was sure they would be sensible, but even she knew that in Matthew they had a great and very deadly weapon.

"You know; James doesn't always have Matthew murder everyone. Just a few people and they were trying to kill either him or me at the time."

"Justified killings then." Sophie chuckled.

"Of course."

Sophie had developed a close relationship with her sister-in-law. They spoke to each other on the phone several times a week and used What's App to ping messages all day. She hated not being around Thomas all the time, but thanks to Skype, she saw and spoke to him lots. LA was her home now, and that would never change. She loved it there. Well, she did until the article broke. Would it ever be the same again?

"Do you know what James is doing?" She asked Amy.

"I know bits. Trust them. It'll be alright." Amy took Sophie's hands and squeezed them when she replied.

"I do." The two of them embraced.

"Hey, can we get in on the love-in." Sonia wrapped her arms around the two of them.

"Girls rule," Marie giggled out and joined.

"Girls are in a lot of trouble." Matthew's gruff voice came from behind Sophie. They all jumped apart and stood in a line. James, Matthew, Callum and Grayson all filed into the shop wearing frowns that had Sophie's bottom smarting already.

"We...er..." Sonia tried to answer, but the growl from Matthew silenced her.

"Carl, Damian." Grayson stepped forward.

"Yes, boss." They both cowered.

"You are relieved of your duties for the day. You may go back to Mr North's home."

"Yes, Sir." Both men couldn't get out the place quickly enough.

"Sophie." Grayson turned his attention to her. She stepped forward. They were still in the armoury. Everyone around them went quiet. "Do you remember your safe word?"

"Yes, Master." The games were about to start

"Ladies, how about you?" Grayson addressed Marie, Amy, and Sonia.

"Yes, Master Grayson." They all replied in unison. Grayson nodded at the other men. They all had that look on their faces that meant by the end of the night Sonia, Marie, Amy and herself would be left thoroughly sated.

"Good because we have four very disobedient little submissives to punish."

CHAPTER TWELVE

Grayson

"Slave position. Now." The tone of Grayson's voice left Sophie, Marie and Sonia in no doubt of what was about to happen. He couldn't believe that Sophie had gone out with the girls and was even more incredulous that it was her idea. He told her to stay in James' mansion, and she defied him. James took Amy to his London home, they had their playroom there, but Grayson, along with Matthew and Callum came to the club that Grayson owns in London. At least that one hadn't been destroyed by a rioting crowd. The club was empty, apart from them; a definite benefit to owning such a place.

All three women knelt before them naked with their heads bowed.

"The club safe word is red; you all have your individual safe words. If you are not sure about anything to use them. Do you understand?"

"Yes, Master Grayson." A chorus of female voices replied.

"Sonia, you are more experienced with play of this nature and Sophie you're a full time submissive. Would you help Marie with anything that she does not understand?" Callum stepped forward. Grayson knew that the Prime Minister's son was an expert in the art of Domination and Submission, but his wife was relatively new to it and still learning.

"We will do all we can to help her." Sophie and Sonia agreed.

"Do you know why you are to be punished?" Matthew spoke this time.

"Because you told us to stay in the house, and we went

shopping for Drew," Sonia replied. Matthew stepped forward and twisted his hand around Sonia's ponytail. He pulled her head up until she was looking at him. "Nothing to do with Rascal's cakes and filling that beautiful belly of yours."

"Maybe." She pouted at him.

"I don't think my girl is remorseful for her actions at all, Grayson. She seems to think that she isn't my pet to do with what I like."

"I have a feeling Sophie and Marie feel the same way. Don't you Callum?" Grayson smirked. The play was underway and the skin on his arms pricked up with the allure of what was to come. They decided together what they would do with the women on the way to collect them.

"I think we need to remind them." Callum turned and pulled a length of hemp rope from his bag. This had been Grayson's idea; he was a shibari master. They would dress their women in the beautiful ropes, restrain them so that they could do whatever they wanted.

"Amber," Marie called out. They all stopped, and Callum knelt beside his wife. "Talk to me."

"I'm worried about the baby."

Callum looked up at Grayson to answer this question.

"We will not be tying ropes in any way that will harm the baby. Only Sophie will be suspended." His little submissive wiggled her bottom in delight to hear that one.

"You won't leave me alone the entire time?" Marie looked up to Callum. Her soulful eyes wide with wanting to try but fear for the safety of her unborn.

"Darling, I'll be in you most of the time, so believe me, I'm not going anywhere." Callum's reply brought a chuckle to Grayson's lips. He planned on being the same with Sophie.

"Ok." The brunette smiled. "Let's do it."

Callum rewarded her with a kiss on the lips.

Grayson turned to Matthew. The bodyguard was standing behind Sonia and was already binding her arms together. Matthew was also an expert at this. They had both worked together in their training and had taken turns in tying each other up. It wasn't something they spoke about between them. Although Grayson did have to admit he felt less on edge around the big man when he was restricted.

He took his own length of rope.

"On your feet little one."

Sophie stood up. She placed her palms flat to her thighs.

"I've taught you well. Let's see about securing those hands so they can't play. He made a loop and thread it around her hand. The fabric of the rope was soft to touch; she would feel it against her skin, but it wouldn't cut her. He pulled the rope around her body and then fastened the other hand.

"That should keep you from pleasuring yourself for a few minutes." Grayson looked over to Matthew and Callum; each had withdrawn to a corner of the room. Callum was already building an intricate pattern of beautiful knots between Marie's thighs and up her backside.

"I think my little one needs ties in those places." He caught Sophie watching also. "You always were a voyeur. I think I'm going to have to blindfold you to keep that concentration on me."

"I'm sorry, Master." Sophie smirked with delight.

He pulled a silk scarf from his bag and tied it around her eyes. "That should focus your attention a little better. Next, he worked his knots between her thighs and bottom. He paid particular attention to her clit with a beautiful rose adorning it.

"You smell amazing already." He inhaled deeply and then blew out. The little gusts of air from his breath sending waves of dancing delight over her highly sensitised skin. He needed to taste her. To sup at the glistening desire that was evident between her thighs. The wet tip of his tongue traced her inner folds, flicked over her clit and then swirled around her opening.

"Mmm." She moaned and dug the tips of her fingernails

into her hips.

"You like that?"

"Yes, Master."

He wasn't going any further just yet though. He still had a lot of rope left and his wife needed to be suspended for the next part of his plan. She was placing a lot of trust in him, and he would reward her with his complete devotion. The rope was looped around and ankle and back up her calf. He brought it back down the other leg then straight back up to her breasts. The fibres of the rope bristled together in the silence of the room. None of the other couples made a sound as each man concentrated on adorning his woman with the most beautiful of natural tethers. He knew that Sophie had a sensitive spot just above her bottom, so he finished his knots there. She wiggled with the feelings pulsating through her body. He placed a hand over the knot on her back, and she let out a long lust filled moan.

"It's time to string you up."

"Please Master." There was a very keen edge to Sophie's voice. Grayson loved how she embraced her submission when she was with him. There was no hesitation or worry. She trusted that he would not hurt her; she trusted him to bring her great pleasure. Since the day he first saw her looking out at the Hollywood hills, he knew she would always do that.

He reached above them to where two chains dangled down from the ceiling. They both had hooks on the end of them which he attached to strategically placed knots on Sophie's ropes. One at her shoulders and one between her legs by her knees.

"Brace yourself." On the wall behind him was a button. He pressed it, and the chains shortened lifting his stunning creation into the air. He needed out of his jeans at the vision before him. He created his very own goddess. Sophie breathlessly mewed. The tension of the rope was pulling on each of the sensitive spots dotted around her skin. She swayed; her head fell forward as she became enveloped in the feelings flooding through her body.

"Oh, no. Time to bring you back to consciousness." He took a vibrating butt plug and smothered it in lubrication. He made a design in his ropes that allowed him to pull on the end of a length, and it would adjust Sophie's legs to just how he wanted them. He pulled it. She gasped. She was now splayed open for him to do with as he wished.

Matthew and Callum brought their woman back over to where they were.

"Please Master, when Drew is out can we do that?" Sonia's eyes were wide open with envy.

"If I can flog you while you're up there." The bodyguard raised an eyebrow.

"Have you got your toys?" Grayson asked both men.

"Already in." Callum smacked Marie on the back side, and she let out a loud groan where Grayson guessed her butt plug was already situated.

"On all fours on the chair my love." Matthew held up Sonia's toy, and she obliged him. Grayson ran his hand over Sophie's glistening folds and brought her juices back to her puckered hole. He then tenderly pushed the lubricated plug in. She shuddered with the intrusion.

"Tell me how you are feeling?" He whispered into her ear.

"Like I need more, Master."

"More?"

"I want you to fill me everywhere. Show me that you are the boss, and I need to do as I'm told. Use my body. It's yours to take."

"Fuck. You'll be the death of me one day."

"I hope not, Master." She giggled.

"You disobeyed my order today. That means you don't get my manhood inside this tight little pussy." He stuck a finger inside her for emphasis. The ropes swung her so that she was fucking his finger. "You'll get to suck me till you swallow all my cum though. This cunt is getting a substitute." He pulled a thickly ridged vibrator from his bag.

Matthew and Callum did the same. Sophie and Marie gasped. Grayson was in charge now. He was dominating the group towards their inevitable climaxes. This was the role he took over the others. He relished it. He'd wasted so long in mindless sexual escapes, just to get his kicks, when all he needed to do was play tutor to Dom's with his special little goddess.

"Master, please, I want to see. I promise to pay attention to only you." Sophie whimpered out. He placed the vibrator down and came to Sophie's head. He pulled her head up and whipped the blindfold off.

"Me, you focus only on me."

"You, only you." Her eyes gave him the promise he needed. He picked up the vibrator; she followed him with her gaze. She gasped, and the ropes shook again. The tight knots heightened the absolute pleasure in her body.

"Please. Please." He loved it when she begged.

In a tantalising thrust, he settled the vibrator into her tight haven. She cried out at the intrusion.

"Full. So full." He smirked at her passionate retort. Marie and Sonia were also panting with their thirst for climax.

"Matthew do you have the other jewels that I asked for?"

"More?" Marie called out.

"Always more," Callum replied to her. "No more words unless it's you screaming my name."

"Yes, Master." The brunette was new to BDSM, but she was well trained already. A natural when she forgot her nerves.

"No clit is complete unless it is adorned with a beautiful little butterfly." Matthew handed Grayson and Callum clit clips. Grayson applied his to Sophie and stood back to watch his bejewelled beauty. The toys were all highlighted by the rope. All he needed to do now was turn them all on.

"Do you think out ladies have learnt their lesson yet?" Matthew chuckled.

All three women nodded.

"I'm not actually sure they have." Grayson held up a remote and pressed the on button.

"Fuck!" Sophie called out as all the devices attached to her started to vibrate at once. She jerked, and that sent her swinging on the ropes. "Oh God!" She let out a loud out on a long, long sob.

"No, just your husband." Grayson laughed as he observed Matthew and Callum press their buttons, and the other two girl's eyes lit up.

"Now, we have two holes filled. But I do believe that there is a third. And that is the one that got them all into so much trouble. That is the one that does all the talking about disobeying us." Matthew mused.

"That is the one that would have eaten all the cakes," Callum added.

"So that is the one that gets to eat something else." Grayson was already pulling his jeans to the floor while he spoke. His cock rejoiced at the freedom it was being given. He stroked up and down his length which brought a welcoming whimper from Sophie's lips. "Time to pleasure your Master."

All three men now had their dicks out and were feeding them into the warm and welcoming mouths of their partners. Sophie's mouth was always delectable. He instantly went to the back of her throat as he knew she could take him. She licked around the rim, around the length and backed down again. He didn't need to move. All he had to do was give the ropes a gentle push, and everything was done for him. His wife was swinging backwards and forwards, and her mouth was caressing up and down his cock. He pulled out when she swung back again.

"You don't come until you feel me come down your throat; do you hear me?"

"Yes, Master," Sophie replied; her wide eyes darkened with desire, looking directly up at him. Sonia and Matthew, Callum and Marie were all lost in their worlds of euphoria. It was time for him and Sophie to lose themselves in theirs. He turned up the button on the vibrator, Sophie screamed out his name, and he rammed his dick back in her mouth. This time he wasn't gentle. This time he needed resolution. He fucked her mouth like it would be the last thing he ever did. He was using her as a toy to get off, and he saw in the flushing of her face and vibrations of her throat around his cock that she loved it. She loved giving herself over so completely, perfect trust, perfect pleasure. His balls tightened, and the warmth of his orgasm rushed through his body and out into his wife's mouth. She detonated around his dick; her entire body was convulsing as she shook so violently with her orgasm her eyes rolled back in her head. She was flying high; he'd taken her to subspace. The pride settled well on his shoulders. He watched her, another press of the button and she came again. His legs collapsed when he released himself from her mouth with a pop. He fell to the floor trying to catch his breath. Sophie hung limply in the ropes. She was completely out of it. He gathered himself together. In an instant, he had stopped the vibrators and removed them. He lowered the chains so that she was resting on the floor. He unhooked them and took a pair of scissors from his bag. The ropes were snipped, and she was in his arms in less than a minute. Matthew and Callum took their women to quiet corners for aftercare. Grayson pulled Sophie on his lap when he sat on a sofa. A blanket rested there, and he covered them both with it.

"Talk to me little one." He needed to check she was ok and coming back into her body alright.

She let out a contented moan.

"Thank you, Master."

"Thank you for trusting me."

"Always." Her words sounded so dreamy, as she began to drift off to sleep.

"Will you go out again when I've asked you not to?"

"Not this week?" She laughed before drifting off.

CHAPTER THIRTEEN

Sophie

Sophie placed the magazine article down. No matter how many times she read it, she never tired of taking delight in the content and especially the photograph that accompanied it. The loathsome Sally Bridgewater being thrown out of the London Daily headquarters. Apparently, she created a storm of colourful language when fired and threw things at the Editor in Chief. She had to be ejected from the premises. Sophie thought that it couldn't have happened to a nicer person.

"Mrs Moore." Sophie looked up to see Mrs Aimes, the housekeeper, standing before her.

"How can I help you?"

"I was just about to start preparing dinner, but I need a few things. I'm going to head to town. Do you need anything before I go?"

"No. I'm going to have a little sleep before Grayson gets back."

The sun was rising by the time they got back to the mansion after the club scenes the previous evening. Grayson had a few hours sleep and then headed back to London for business meetings. Sophie's body ached pleasantly. Their scene was so intense but just what they needed after the tension of the last few days.

Mrs Aimes left Sophie alone. She threw the newspaper article in the bin. It was time to move on and forget that woman. With a spring in her step, she leapt up the stairs to her bedroom. The room was decorated in princess style. She had antique French furniture with light pink accents on the wall. The room was dominated by a massive chandelier. It was the bedroom of her dreams; James had always said that he would make her such a room one day. He had kept his word. She lay on the bed and instantly drifted off to a peaceful slumber.

A short time later, Sophie woke by her bedroom door opening. She glanced at the clock, three pm. Grayson was home early. She sat up and rubbed her eyes. The figure at her bedside emerging from the hazy sleep though was not her husband; it was Sally Bridgewater.

"Miss Bridgewater." Sophie leapt from the bed and reached for her phone on the nightstand. However, before she could get it, Sally grabbed it and threw it across the room at the wall.

"I don't think so." Sally spat out. The droplets of saliva hit her in the face. "You and I need to have a little talk about your husband. Sophie noticed that Sally had red rims around her puffy eyes; she'd either been crying or hadn't slept. She imagined it was both.

"Any questions you have need to be addressed directly to Grayson. Get out! There will be people here soon."

"I don't think so. Your husband is in London, and the estate steward had to leave to assist his wife who strangely seemed to get a puncture. The bodyguard left behind really needs to watch what he drinks. I don't think he'll be waking anytime soon." Sally cackled.

Sophie gulped; her whole skin prickling at the apparently insane woman's words.

"Sally, I know what happened yesterday, but you being here will only make matters worse. If you leave now, I won't tell anyone you were here."

"Not enough," Sally screamed while rocking on the spot. "Over here...NOW." Sophie didn't want to aggravate the woman anymore. It was evident that reasoning was not going to work; she feared Miss Bridgewater's brain was too far gone for that. She followed Sally's direction and sat down at a little table that had been rescued from a French Chateaux before it was demolished. It was placed by the window with two chairs. Sally let out a bellowing laugh.

"So this is what it feels likes for Grayson when he is bossing you around. I think I like this power. I wonder what else I can get you to do." The evil smirk on Sally's face brought bile to her mouth. "Don't worry. I'm not into women. That is the whole reason I'm here and ready to destroy your husband." Sally said before taking the seat opposite her. Sophie hadn't seen it before but on the table was a folder. She really didn't want to know what was in it but had a feeling she was about to find out.

"Just tell me what it is you want and then leave."

"Sally pushed the folder towards her.

"Open it."

"You open it." She retorted.

"Open it or things are going to get interesting." With a shaking hand, Sophie reached out and pulled the file towards her. She opened the front cover to reveal a baby.

"Who is this? She asked.

"My son."

"So that's what you want, to guilt trip us. You went after my husband with lies." She didn't need to hear this, so she slammed her chair back and stood up. "Get out."

"That was my son as a baby." Sally ignored her and flipped over another page. "And this is my son, now five, a few weeks ago."

The bottom fell out of Sophie's world when she looked down at the piece of paper. The eyes, the hair colour, the face that stared back was that of Grayson.

"No." She wrapped her arms around her body to try and shut out the pain.

"Yes, my son is also Grayson's."

"You're lying."

More pages were turned and a birth certificate was revealed. Sally shoved it in her face. Sophie's heart told her not to believe all the evidence, but her brain rationalised everything and said she had to believe it. She sat back down and picked up the picture of the little boy.

"How?"

"I played a groupie for a scoop on Mr Moore's sex skills. I'm sure you already know I will do anything for a story. Unfortunately, I was not as careful as I should have been with my pills; the flights messed me up, and the condom broke. I didn't want to believe I was pregnant at first. Me, pregnant that couldn't be happening." Sally shifted in her chair as if the memories of her disgrace were more painful than anything else. "By the time I admitted it, I was too late for a termination. I had to give birth to the bastard. Thankfully his new family took him straight away, so I didn't even have to look at him. Unfortunately, I got sent that photo."

"Why didn't you tell Grayson?"

"He had just announced his relationship with you, including the whole leading you around by the collar thing at that party. I was disgusted. That was the man who had put this thing inside me. But do you know the worse part? Mr Smith won't publish my article on Grayson. I told him that we could really get a good story out of it. I could see the headline." Sally's eyes glazed over as she held her hand up to her chance at stardom. "Renegade star doesn't use protection. How many more bastards does he have out there?" It was shut down, and I was sent away to have the child. It was the one time in my life that I messed up, and for what, a quick fuck that wasn't even that good?"

"We would've helped you if you'd come to us." Sophie offered.

"I don't need your pity." Sally slammed the folder shut. "That article was mine; I should have been allowed to publish it. I was punished for your husband's misdemeanours. He was the one who should have been lambasted for fucking anything that walked. He is a disgrace to his roots. I'm glad I did that article with his sister."

"You don't know Grayson well. He isn't the man you paint him to be."

"And you are blind." Sally interrupted her when she was about to try and defend her husband. "And I'm not going to rest until I destroy him. It will make me the greatest reporter there has ever been. Your brother's little plot will fail. I will expose the lot of you for the freaks that you are." Sally grabbed the folder back from her and jumped to her feet.

"I won't allow you to do that. Sally, you need help. I can help you." It was evident now that somewhere along the line, Sally had lost her mind." Sophie made her own attempt to retake the folder of the fast retreating woman.

"Get the fuck off me." Sally pushed her and Sophie stumbled backwards against the table. Her hip caught on it, and a pain ripped through her left leg. Sally made a beeline for the door. Sophie knew that she needed to keep the women in the room. If she got out, if she got out then their lives, Amy's and James' lives, would all be exposed. Would Sally find out that her brother had killed people? He would be sent to prison. Grayson could be hurt; she could lose him. She couldn't allow that to happen. In a quick movement, she ignored the pain in her leg and was on top of Sally before she reached the door. She ripped the folder from the shocked reporter's hands and threw it across the room. The contents spilt out everywhere.

"You bitch." Sally turned and sent a punch straight into Sophie's face who managed to recover from it quickly and returned her own punch.

"You are not going anywhere. You need help, and I'm going to make sure you get it."

"I need to destroy anyone involved with the North family. I know what you are like. You all use your money to think you are above the law. Grayson, your brother, his bodyguard, and the Prime Minister's son." They were both grappling together on the floor. "I'll destroy everyone." Sally sent a kick to her stomach, and before Sophie had a chance to react, the reporter was on her feet and racing for the door. She managed to reach her hand out and grab Sally's trailing leg though. The reporter went down straight onto the edge of a sturdy wooden dressing table. Her head cracked with a sickening thud, and she slumped down onto the floor unmoving. Sophie got to her to check. The reporter had blood pouring from a wound to her head.

"Sally?"

Nothing.

"Sally?" Sophie couldn't see her breathing. She'd killed her. It was an accident, but she'd killed her. What should she do? She looked around the room. Furniture was upended, and the paper was everywhere. The evidence of Grayson's misdemeanours with the reporter. It was accidental. She hadn't meant to do it. She just wanted to stop her from leaving. The police, she needed to call them. No, an ambulance, maybe she wasn't dead. She was going to be sick; air, she needed air. Without actually thinking, Sophie left the room, her brain a maelstrom of confusion. Had she just killed someone? She was shaking. Stepping into the ornate porch of the mansion, she bent over and was violently sick everywhere. Heaving again and again 'til nothing was left. She was going to go to prison. She murdered someone. The mother of Grayson's child. She heaved again. Think. She hit herself on the head, trying in vain to get her brain to start functioning. It didn't work so she slumped down and curled up into a little ball. Her life as she knew it was over.

The sound of a car engine brought her consciousness back to focus. She instantly recognised that car as the one that James used when in Yorkshire. Matthew slammed on the brakes and skidded to a halt as the car got to the entrance to the house. Matthew and James both leapt out.

"Sophie." Her brother called. Matthew pulled a gun from his pocket and primed it. James was at her side checking for injuries. "Where is she?"

"You know what I did? How?" She looked at him through now fatigued eyes.

"Matthew has been tracking Sally. As soon as we saw she was on the way here, we got here as fast as we could."

"She's inside," Sophie replied. James looked at Matthew, a quizzical eyebrow raised.

"Sophie. What happened?"

"She's dead." The emotion in her voice was flat. She felt

as if she were in a dream. That nothing happening around her was real. Matthew disappeared into the house.

"Sophie, let's get you inside. You can't stay out here."

"No." She didn't want to go back to her room. Her nails dug tightly into James' hand.

"It's alright. You don't have to go to your room, but I do need to get you into the house. It's getting cold out here, and I don't want you to get sick." She nodded at her brother, and he picked her up and carried her into the house. He settled her on a chaise lounge in the hallway. Matthew appeared at the top of the stairs. He coughed, and they both looked up at him. The bodyguard shook his head.

"Sophie, I need to know that happened?" James focused her attention back on him.

"We fought, and she fell. She was going to destroy us all." She was almost hyperventilating, trying to get the words out.

"Alright. I need you to stay calm. Matthew will deal with Miss Bridgewater."

"I'm going to go to prison. I'll be charged with murder." She was the opposite of calm; she was terrified. She clung to her brother's shirt.

"Little sis. You know I won't allow that to happen." Matthew came to the top of the stairs again and whistled for James to join him. "I've just got to speak to Matthew. You stay here. When I get back, I'll get you a stiff drink." He rubbed her shoulders; she was still shivering. "And I'll get a blanket to keep you warm."

She nodded, and her eyes followed James up the stairs and to Matthew. They lowered their voices so she couldn't hear them, but she knew exactly what was being said when Matthew passed the photo to James. He put it in the pocket of his suit trousers before disappearing into her bedroom. He reappeared a few minutes later and descended the stairs to wrap the blanket around her shoulders. He pressed a kiss to the top of her forehead then went into the lounge to pour a huge glass of brandy. He helped her to drink it down. The warm liquid calmed and centred her.

"Thank you."

"That's alright little sis. I don't employ an ex-MI5 agent for no reason. You won't go to prison. Matthew will make her death look like a suicide."

"But I killed her."

"She was never here Sophie, so how could you have killed her?" The look on his face told her that she shouldn't argue with him; he was protecting her.

"Alright. But what do I tell Grayson?"

"I'll talk to him for you. As far as he will be concerned, she committed suicide on our premises. You found her, and it upset you. Matthew moved her body away from here to avoid a publicity circus. It's what has to happen Sophie. Do you understand that?"

"You won't tell him that I killed her?" She bit her lip with worry over the lie.

"I think it's best not to." He reached for the photo in his pocket. "Does he know?"

She shook her head.

"I only found out when she came here and showed me the photo. She was about to expose the story to the press. I tried to stop her from leaving the room. She hit me; I hit her back. We fought, and she fell onto the table. I didn't mean to kill her." She had her brother's hands held really tightly, so tightly, in fact, that his knuckles turned white from the pressure. "I just knew she couldn't leave the room. I was trying to lock her in so I could call you and Grayson."

"I know. Shush. Don't worry. It will be alright."

"What should I do about the boy?"

"We need to find him and check that he is Grayson's."

"Look at him." She pointed at the picture.

"I know, but looks can be deceiving. Sally Bridgewater did anything for a story. That's been proven a million times. I will have Matthew find the boy, and we can do a DNA test. We can then break the news to Grayson, when we know the truth. He is apprehensive about the slur on his ancestry and neglect of culture. He needs to come to terms with his thoughts on that first. Finding out he has a child could send him spiralling even more."

"I want to protect him. I love him but to lie to him?" She didn't think she could do that.

"Sophie, you have to trust me on this. We will tell Grayson eventually. We just need to ensure that everything is alright first."

What could she do? Her brother was rescuing her from prison on a charge of murder. She wasn't in control of her situation anymore. That little boy would haunt her for the rest of her life. Grayson had a child with another woman, and Sophie had murdered the mother. She shut her eyes and let the tears out. She let them flow for the end of her life as she had known it. She'd been protected and sheltered, carefree and alive. Something inside her died today; it would never be replaced. It would never be the same.

CHAPTER FOURTEEN

Grayson

A MONTH LATER

Grayson slammed his fist into the boxing punch bag. He'd been hitting it for an hour now and still didn't feel like he had expelled all the anger that he held inside him. That damn woman. Even in her death, she was still haunting them. That day, when he returned from London, he found his wife broken and distraught. Sally Bridgewater had put a gun to her head where she knew that Sophie would find her. He'd insisted on seeing the body to know that she was indeed dead. There wasn't much of her head left given she'd used a shotgun. He hoped she rotted in Hell.

Sophie came into the gym in their LA mansion. She had on her gym gear; day after day, she seemed to just run on the treadmill for hours. His wife withdrew into herself. He offered to get her a counsellor to help her through the worse of her emotions, but she'd stated that she was fine and that she was reconciling them on her own. He used his Dom voice to try and convince her, he even brought a counsellor to the house, but she still refused help. The only person she seemed to talk to about everything was James. The dynamic of their relationship had changed. She had to blame him. It was the only reason she was shutting him out.

He watched her build up to a fast pace. The bones were jutting out on her back she had lost so much weight. This shell wasn't his wife anymore. He pulled off his boxing clothes and put them away. He was covered in sweat from all his efforts. A cold shower was just what he needed. And he made the decision that his wife was going to join him. He went to the front of her running machine. She looked up at him and pressed the button to slow down.

"No exercising for you today little one. I've got other things planned for you." She brought the machine to a halt but didn't stop. "I want you naked in the shower in five minutes. I'm going examine every inch of your body to see how much weight you have lost. I'm then going to fuck it until you remember I'm your master. After that, we are going out for food, and you will eat all that I tell you to. Do you understand?"

She looked at him and bowed her head.

"Red." The word from her lips took him aback. He reached out to a cross trainer behind so that he didn't fall.

"Red?"

"Red." She repeated.

"To all of it?" He sounded like a complete idiot, but he was utterly bewildered.

"Yes."

"Why?"

"I want to run." That was her reason. She wanted to run.

"You do too much running. Sophie, you are losing to much weight. I'm worried about you." Despite the fact he was sweaty, he pulled her into his arms to show her his affection. She didn't relax into his comfort. Instead, she remained rigid like a statue. "I know this is my fault. My past made that woman do what she did. You need to let me help you so I can make it up to you." Sophie wriggled out of his arms.

"I'm going lay down. I don't feel well." With that comment, she left the room at a run. It was as though she couldn't even stand to be near him. His marriage was breaking down before his very eyes, and he didn't know how to fix it. He loved her so much; he wanted his wife back. Damn his male slut ways. They were the reason for this. He managed to convince his Native American heritage of his true intentions to help them, and the new community centre was halfway completed already. Had he lost his wife in the process though? He needed to speak to the one person who knew Sophie just as well as he did. Her brother.

Grayson quickly showered and entered his study. He shut the door so Sophie couldn't hear him. She'd curled up in their bed and had fallen asleep so that shouldn't be a problem anyway. He dialled.

"James North." His brother in law sleepily answered.

"Hi, it's Grayson." He replied.

"What's up. It's two am here." Shit, he forgot about the time difference.

"Fuck, I'm sorry man. I'll call you back tomorrow." He could hear Amy murmur in the background, and James tell her to go back to sleep.

"It's alright." Grayson could hear James get out of bed and walk to a different room and shut the door. "It's not like you to forget the time difference, so you obviously need to talk."

"I'm worried about Sophie." There he had said it. "She just safe worded."

"Safe worded. Do I want to hear about this?"

"I asked her to shower with me which would have led to..."

James interrupted him with a 'la la la'.

"Sorry, I told her after the shower we were going to head out for food."

James went silent for a moment.

"She safe worded because you wanted to shower and eat with her?"

"Yes. James, if you saw her... All she does all day is sleep and run. I've tried to feed her like I normally do, but she only has a few bites before she ambers. She's lost so much weight. I called in a counsellor, but she wouldn't speak to them. I know she talks to you a lot; has she said anything?" He felt a great weight lift off his chest as he confided in some else his fears.

"She's said a few things. I know what happened has affected her. She probably just needs times. Sophie's always been a sensitive soul. You knew that when you married her.

She's probably still just petrified that you're going to get hurt." James' reply was reassuring, but he was at the stage that he needed more.

"I think there is more to it. She's not even really spoken to me about what happened that day. What has she said to you?"

"Look, Grayson, how about I talk to her? I'll give her a call tomorrow and see what she says. If I think there is something major wrong then I'll fly over, and we'll stage an intervention together. I know you're worried about her that makes me concerned."

"That would be great. I have to head to Navajo territory tomorrow. I have a photo shoot for the community project I'm doing there. I did ask her to come with me, but she said no. She'll be home all day." Grayson was actually worried about leaving her, but he really wanted to be involved with the projects, he had going on in his homelands, as much as possible. They accepted his reasons for not being seen to be helping in the past, and he was building many bridges in the area.

"I'll call her and have a long chat then."

"Thank you, James."

"Not a problem. Leave Sophie for today. We'll get this sorted. Night."

"Night." Grayson hung up and relaxed back in his office chair. For the first time in weeks, he felt the tension evaporate from his shoulders. He let out a long breath. On his desk was a picture of him and Sophie on their wedding day. He picked it up and stroked his wife's face. She was his saviour, his angel. She got him and his needs and wasn't ashamed of her own. They were a match made in heaven. He wouldn't allow Sally Bridgewater to drag them down to her type of hell. He placed the picture back down on his desk and rubbed his eyes. Maybe it was time to join his wife for sleep. He wouldn't pressure her into anything. He just wanted her to know that he was there for her to help her. He ambled into the bedroom and stood against the door frame. Sophie was on her back with her long blonde hair fanned over the bed. She looked like an angel, peaceful and sleeping. She moaned and thrashed to her side. Her little face scrunched up.

"Stop it." She called out.

"Sophie." He stepped forward in concern. She didn't wake but threw herself onto the other side of the bed.

"I didn't mean to do it. It was an accident. I had to stop her. Please." She called out.

"Accident, stop who?" Grayson was getting more and more worried by the minute. He placed his arms on Sophie's shoulders and shook her. She startled awake, took one look at him and scrambled from the bed. She ran into the bathroom, and when he followed her, he saw she was sick in the toilet. He took a facecloth from the side and wet it. Sophie was covered in sweat and shaking.

"Little one what happened?"

She burst into tears, and his heart started to break. He hated to see her like this. His past had harmed her in ways that he could never stop from hurting. Damn that reporter. He was her master and was supposed to be protecting her, but at the moment, he was weak and not able to do that. He was failing.

"Bad dream." She sobbed.

"What about?" He questioned.

"I...I..." She hesitated. "I don't want to talk about it."

"Sophie. What was an accident?" He stroked the hair back from her face to calm her down.

"I'm sorry." She blinked up at him.

"You were calling out in your sleep. You said you didn't mean it to happen. It was an accident, and you had to stop her? Who was her? Please tell me what is going on."

His wife went as white as a sheet, sobbed 'I can't' and placed her head back into the toilet to be sick again. There was nothing more that he could do. She shut him out again, but he stayed with her just holding her hair back. All he could do was pray that James could get some answers.

CHAPTER FIFTEEN

Sophie

Her stomach hurt so much from where she spent hours being sick. Nothing stayed down. She felt dizzy where her body was so weak. She was living in a nightmare and couldn't escape. Every time she shut her eyes, she saw Sally's face looking up at her. Her eyes dead pools of nothingness. She, Sophie had done that. She'd killed someone, and now she was lying to her husband. She would burn in the afterlife for this. Grayson reluctantly left her earlier that morning to head to the Navajo territory. He left the phone beside her and told her to call him if she needed him at all. She could see the guilt on his face. He blamed himself for the way she was. She was cruel to him, but she needed to listen to her brother. Why wouldn't this pain go away?

The phone rang, she looked down at the caller ID, it was her brother. She answered and immediately burst into tears.

"Sophie?"

"Yes." She cried.

"Put the phone on a video call. I need to see you."

"No." She replied.

"Please, little sis." There was sadness in her brother's voice. She switched the call and held the phone in front of her. "Fuck," James exclaimed when he saw her face. She knew she looked awful. Her eyes were sunken in, and her skin was ghostly pale. She had bags under her eyes from where she was so fitful in her sleep. "What have I done?"

"You've done nothing. I'm the one that did this when I murdered Sally Bridgewater." Her reply was devoid of all emotion.

"No, listen to me. That was an accident."

"Matthew shot her in the head."

"She was already dead; she didn't feel anything." He tried to reason with her.

"They had to use fingerprints to identify her." She shuddered at the thought. In most of her dreams, Sally morphed from the woman who she had tried to reason with into a horrific vision of blood and torn flesh. An eye dangled by a thread from its socket taunting her for her crimes. Then, the little boy would appear, calling for his daddy.

"Sophie, it needed to be done to save you. I'm not going to let you feel guilty for what happened after you left that room. That was my and Matthew's decision. Any guilt is Matthew's and mine."

"That is easier said than done when she haunts my dreams," Sophie screamed into the phone.

"I know." James' voice was kind, but the underlying tone was one of control, "But you have to move on. Matthew is on his way to you now. He's bringing my doctor. You're to listen to whatever she says and take whatever medicine she gives you. No arguments. Do you hear me?"

"I don't need pills, I need answers."

"And we are getting them," James shouted down the phone at her. She could see he was getting frustrated. "Look, I'm not just sending Matthew to see you. He has found the boy. Matthew is going to do a DNA test to ensure that he's Grayson's. Then we can tell him. The waiting is nearly over. You just have to get it together and hold steady for a few more days. Be the strong girl I know that you can." James paused. He ran his hand through his hair. "Be the one who supported me after I was beaten. Do you remember that Sophie? At the hospital. I remember you talking to me when I was sleeping. Telling me that you loved me, and I wasn't to listen to what I'd been called. I was a great brother and a good person. Kind and so helpful. I only got through those first days because of you. If you hadn't been there, I would have probably killed myself.

"Please don't" She wept.

"Yes. You are a real person, Sophie. None of this is your

fault. It was an accident. Sally was not a nice person; she was deranged. She gave away her child, Grayson's child. She never allowed him to know of his son. The more digging I've done on her, the more I've found out what she was willing to do for a story. Sleeping with Grayson seems angelic compared to some. Sophie, she injected her own mother with heroin to watch her die from an overdose. You have rid the world of a menace. Grayson's son would have been in danger as long as she lived."

"What?" She silenced her crying, her voice caught in her throat as she tried to find words for what she was hearing. "She...she killed her own mother?"

"It could never be proven. She was clever but yes. Matthew is hundred percent sure of that."

"I'm losing my mind over a person who had no heart."

"Yes. Neither a heart nor a soul, she sold that to the Devil years ago" Her brother's face softened.

"Grayson is anxious about me isn't he?"

"He phoned me yesterday in the middle of the night. He said you safe-worded. As much as I don't like to know what my little sister gets up to in her sex life, I know you've never done that before. It worried us both."

"He wanted me to be normal. I got so scared the way he was looking at me. I've been lying to him."

"To protect him. He'll understand."

"Will he?"

"Sophie. He loves you. We did what we needed to do at the time to protect you. He will know that when we can all sit down and explain. I'm getting a plane over tomorrow. Amy and I had a check-up at the doctor's today, so I didn't want to miss that."

"Is everything alright?" Her worry turned instantly to her pregnant sister-in-law.

"Yes, just a regular check but I like to attend them."

She could feel herself calming down and centring. She'd been so stressed with everything, but now she actually felt like she could cope. And maybe even eat something. Some goat's milk pancakes. She wondered if Grayson would make them for her when he got home.

"What are you thinking?" James asked. She must have completely spaced out for the call.

"Pancakes."

"That sounds like the sister who I love."

"Does the boy have a name?" The question suddenly popped into her head from nowhere.

"Grayson's?"

"Yes."

"His adoptive parents have called him Ashkii, Ash for short. It's a Navajo name that means boy. I guess that they knew he had a Native American father."

"I like it. Ash. Suits him. Ashkii Moore."

"Sophie." James interrupted her train of thought. "Don't start thinking of him as yours and Grayson's. There is a long way to go yet. Remember, he believes that the people he lives with are his mother and father."

"He'll never be mine; I know that. I just want Grayson to know about his son."

"He will." Sophie heard Amy call over the phone for pickles. Her sister-in-law's cravings were obviously in full force again. "I better go. Last time I ignored her, I spent a week grovelling."

"Give her and Thomas a cuddle from me." Sophie smiled at her brother's roll of the eyes.

"Bye sis."

She placed the phone down on the bed; she could do this. She could survive. But when she looked up, all she could see was Grayson and thunderous fury written all over his face.

CHAPTER SIXTEEN

Grayson

It was all that he could think about. Getting home to see Sophie. It was the quickest interview he'd ever done and then took the helicopter he rented straight back. He didn't want to leave her at all. She'd cried all night. His wife, helpless, and there was nothing that he could do to help. It wasn't right. He had approached their bedroom and heard her talking. He guessed it was her brother when he heard James voice talking about how she saved him after the attack that left the older North sibling scarred both mentally and physically. That would turn his girl around. She just needed to realise how special she was. The next words out of his brother-in-law's mouth left him reeling though. His world was spinning. The entire conversation between James and Sophie happening in slow motion. He had a child. A son. Ashkii. What the fuck! He'd slept with Sally Bridgewater? Sophie ended the call with James; Grayson stepped forward, and she saw him.

"How much did you hear?" It was the first words from her lips.

"Son." It was all he could say. He needed to sit down, or he was going to fall. He staggered towards the bed. Sophie scrambled across it and tried to touch him. He reeled backwards and chose to sit on a chair instead.

"Grayson, I can explain. Please." She fell out of the bed and onto her knees on the floor in front of him. Her palms rested on her thighs. It was a beautiful slave position. So perfect. But it did not excite him. No, too much was falling into place.

"Accident. James used the same word as you did. What do you mean by it? What was an accident?"

"You have to trust me. Matthew is on his way here. I'll explain everything then."

"No, you won't." He shouted at her. "You will tell me now. You are my wife, and I demand answers."

"Grayson, please. You are in shock at what you heard."

"Your brother said I have a son with Sally Bridgewater. I think I have a fucking right to be shocked; don't you?" He wanted to know what the hell was going on and he wasn't going to rest. "Maybe I need to phone your brother." He stepped over Sophie on the floor and went for her phone.

"No." She was up on her feet and with him. Both of them fighting over the phone. He pushed her away, and she fell down again her dressing table hitting her head in the process. When she sat back up, she had a line of blood falling down her face. She touched it and looked at the crimson life force colouring her hand. Grayson covered his ears when she let out a blood-curdling scream. He was there at her side. Holding her down when she started thrashing wildly around. She was screaming, crying, pleading for mercy.

"I didn't mean to do it. It was an accident. Please, you have to believe me. You have to understand what was happening. She was going to destroy you. She was going to destroy James, Matthew, Callum. All of you. I didn't mean to hurt her."

He shook her to try and snap her out of the fit she was in, but it did not work.

"Sophie." He called. What the fuck was going on? He had a son, Sophie had hurt someone. Sally Bridgewater. He'd gotten her pregnant. He had to calm Sophie down as she was the only one who could tell him what was going on.

He pulled his hand back and slapped it hard around her face. She froze. The blood from her wound was all over them both now.

"You hit me?"

"I needed to do it to calm you down so you can tell me what is going on?"

"I can't." She was pleading with him. Her big brown

eyes were scared.

"Sophie, I'm your husband. We have no secrets from each other."

"I can't tell you, Gray. Please, you have to trust me."

He was done pleading. He wanted answers. He grabbed her by the hair and dragged her to her feet.

"Red, Yellow and Green. Remember." He waited a moment for her to answer.

"Yes, Master."

He had his reply. Without another word, he pulled her through the house to the small playroom that they had installed a few years back.

"Remove all your clothes and lean over the bench."

Sophie did as he asked.

"I want answers, little one, and you are going to give them to me."

"I can't."

"You don't speak unless you are answering my questions." He smacked her hard across the backside. "Understand?"

"Yes, Master." He selected the tool for his task. A wooden paddle. Neither he nor Sophie were masochists. Not like Sonia and Matthew but he needed something strong.

"Sally had a son." He lightly tapped the paddle on her backside, so she knew what was coming if she didn't answer his questions.

"Yes, Master." She replied.

"I'm the father?" He hit her again, this time a little bit harder.

"Yes, Master."

"How?" He hesitated this time, the pain would only come as a reward for an answer.

"She acted a groupie, seduced you for a story on your sex life. She said that the condom broke, and she was remiss with her pill after she'd flown to LA specifically for the story." He rewarded her with a whack.

"Why didn't she tell me?"

"She didn't want to believe she was pregnant until after the time for a termination. We had just begun our relationship then. She had the baby and gave him up for adoption." Sophie was getting more and more breathless with each word. This was the punishment that she craved for all the lies and deceit. He didn't reward her with another paddle this time but just massaged the ache he knew she would be feeling.

"Where is my son. Where is Ashkii?"

"I don't know, but Matthew is on his way to ensure that he is your son."

Thwack.

"What do you mean?" He replied

"Matthew is going to do a DNA test on the boy to ensure that she was not lying. But I know she wasn't. The picture showed me that." Whack

"What picture?" His beat increased.

"She showed me a picture of him. James has it."

His paddle came down hard, this time, as he fought against his temper. They had seen his child, and he hadn't. Sophie screamed out. Grayson placed his hand in between her thighs and pressed down on her clit. She exploded in a violent orgasm. He wasn't finished with her though. He kept his thumb on her now swollen and tender bud.

"When did she show you this picture?"

"The day she died."

"The day she died. She came to see you? You spoke to her?" It suddenly dawned on him. Accident. She didn't mean to. Fuck! "You killed Sally Bridgewater."

He stepped back. Sophie sprung up and covered her body with a nearby towel they used for cleaning up.

"Yes." She tried to flee, but he grabbed her. She'd killed Sally Bridgewater. He must be sick, but the thought made him hard.

"How?"

"She was trying to leave the house. She was going to tell the world you abandoned your child. She said she had proof

James was a killer. She told me she was going to bring down anything related to our families. She'd gone insane." Sophie struggled in his arms.

"Colour."

"Green." He needed to check. This was a game but a deadly serious one. Her reply had him rock hard. He yanked her back onto the bench and lowered his jeans and underwear.

"I'm going to fuck you now."

"Please, Master." She whimpered.

"You are going to tell me exactly what happened while I do." He kicked her legs apart and surged firmly inside her. She cried out and clamped down on his cock. Fuck. He was going to come straight away. "Tell me."

"She tried to escape the room. She hit me, and I hit her back. We ended up rolling around on the floor of my bedroom. Sally got the upper hand and kicked me in the stomach." He withdrew and then slammed back into her. "She got to her feet and tried to run. I had to stop her, so I grabbed her ankle. She fell and hit her head on a wooden unit." Grayson's pace was getting quicker and quicker now. "When I looked at her, she had blood all over her face. She wasn't moving. I panicked and left the room. James and Matthew appeared. Apparently, they were tracking her. They took over and told me what to do." She barely got the last words out before she exploded on his cock, her juices bathing it. He reciprocated and thrust in deep to fill her with his essence.

He collapsed down on top of her. "Including lie to your own husband. Make him feel guilt for something you had done." He pulled out of her. She'd lied to him.

"Grayson." She turned and grabbed his hands. "Please." He pushed her back on the bench.

"You stay there." He pulled up his trousers.

"Where are you going?" She cried, tears filled her eyes.

"I'm going to get my son." He spat back.

"You can't."

"Watch me." He threw the door to their playroom open. Matthew Carter stood the other side. Grayson saw him survey the scene before him. Sophie covered in blood, her ass red raw and cum dripping down her legs.

"Wait." But he never got the rest of the words out before the body guard's big fist knocked him out.

CHAPTER SEVENTEEN

Grayson

"I'm sorry I hit you." Matthew was driving Grayson up the coast of California to San Francisco to meet his son. "I didn't realize you and Sophie did sado-ravishment."

"We don't normally," Grayson replied and continue his embarrassed stare out of the window. "I'm Sophie's, Dom. I needed to do what I did to bring her out of her depression."

"You did well. Although, you're lucky it wasn't James as the door. I think I would've been hiding your body right now. Particularly, since it looked like you were leaving without administering aftercare." Matthew kept his eyes directly ahead of him but raised a telling eyebrow of rebuke.

"Fuck. I was." He groaned. "I guess I got lost in the emotions of the scene as well. I would have left her, if you hadn't had been there. All I could see was that she lied to me."

"Sophie is a full-time submissive, Grayson. I was there after she killed Sally. She was looking for someone to tell her how to act and react. James did what he had to at the time. What he thought was best."

"But to not tell me about my own kid and lie about my wife?" Matthew felt wrong that they had done that. Both should have confided in him straight away.

"James isn't God, although don't tell him I said that. He does make the wrong decisions sometimes. At the time, he was concerned with making sure that his little sister didn't go to jail. I hate to say it, but you probably didn't figure in his decisions." Matthew pulled them off the freeway, as he spoke, and down into the cosmopolitan city. "Sophie couldn't cope with that though. Even though she was just following orders. It's obvious she knows her loyalty lies with you, and it was destroying her. You have got a good one there."

"Have I?" At this point, he wasn't so sure. The woman who loved him had murdered someone and kept that and the fact he had a secret child from him. He wasn't sure that their relationship would ever be the same again. Would he ever actually trust her again? He hadn't even had time to think about Sally's death. How did he feel about that? His wife murdered the mother of his child? He only had Sophie's word on what went on in that room. What if she killed Sally because of the child? Jealousy had consumed her, and she'd struck out? No, that was not the sort of person that Sophie was. He knew her well enough to know that. They had talked about having children, but neither of them were ready yet. With the lifestyle of a twenty-four-seven submissive, it would be difficult. Matthew was right when he said that Sophie needed people to make decisions for her. His wife was the best PA he'd ever had; she was perfect at her job, but she needed him to control her day to day life. She could not do it herself.

"Sally Bridgewater was out to destroy you. I did a sweep of her flat. The woman was obsessed with your destruction, but you weren't the only one. The woman had an obsession with whatever would get her the biggest story. Some of the things that she'd done to get it would have landed her in jail or worse. This was the inevitable end to that woman's life. At least it was quick and merciful."

"You're so practical with death." Grayson watched the straight-faced Matthew as he spoke.

"You mourn her?" Matthew asked

"She's the mother of my child," Grayson replied.

"She's the woman who slept with you for a story. She's the woman who kept the fact she was pregnant with your child. If she hadn't been so blinded, there wouldn't have been a child because she would have aborted it. And when she did finally have the baby, she gave it up without a second thought."

"She must have been scared though?" Grayson couldn't help but try and put himself into Sally's shoes at that time. Matthew pulled the car up to a beautiful Victorian house on the edge of the city. It looked a nice neighbourhood. Cute picket fences and all the gardens were well maintained, houses painted in traditional colours, and neighbourhood watch signs in the windows. This boded well for the life his son had had so far.

"Before you start feeling sorry for her, there is something else you need to know about Sally Bridgewater." Matthew turned the engine off and faced him. His face, usually devoid of emotion unless Sonia was in the room, was covered in anger. "Your son was never officially adopted. This is a foster home. He's been here for a few months now. Before that he was at his adoptive home. Sally didn't want any paperwork that could lead the child back to her, so she sold the kid on the black market. The family he was living with had four other children, all of them were brought up as slaves to the cunts who had bought them. They barely had any food; the clothes that they had were dirty and too small. The eldest, a girl of fifteen, there was evidence of sexual abuse. There was none with your son, but he has seen some horrors. The woman you are worrying about sold him into this and went to the Seychelles on holiday with the money. Do you still feel any remorse for her death?"

The anger flooded through Grayson. He gripped the side of the car so tightly that the whites of his knuckles showed.

"If she weren't dead already, I'd kill the bitch myself." He gritted his teeth together when he spoke. "I hope that the people who dared to do that have been suitably punished."

"They will be."

Grayson's humanity kicked in. "Maybe Sally didn't know about the family."

Matthew snorted a laugh.

"I sometimes forget that you and James have souls that I

lack." He reached for his phone on the dashboard and brought up a copy of a document. Matthew handed the phone to him. "That proves that she knew when the kid was two. She must have had a crisis of conscience, because she searched him out. Did she go to the police with her findings though? No. She planned a story on it. Her only concern was how to make sure nobody found out that the boy was hers. It's why she didn't publish the article, in the end." The last words had barely left Matthew's mouth before Grayson was out of the car. He yelled out and sent his fist into a nearby tree. Curtains twitched and a couple of car alarms started ringing out such was the ferocity of his temper. Matthew was beside him and caught his hand as he went to punch the tree again.

"Your boy is in that house. If he hears you like this, he'll be wary from the start."

"Fucking bitch." He growled

"She'd dead. Sophie did that. She did that for you." Matthew was forever the voice of reason. "You need to pull yourself together."

"You still going to do the DNA test?" He took deep breaths to calm himself down.

"I think we both know the result, even if he isn't yours, but for the sake of the child I will."

He nodded. "I have a son."

The front door to the house opened, and a well-dressed lady stepped out.

"Let's go and meet him."

Grayson brushed the bark from his knuckles. Somehow, he hadn't broken the skin on his hand, but it still stung like a motherfucker.

"Mrs Portillo." Matthew extended his hand to the lady who greeted them. "I'm sorry for the little scene. I'm Matthew Carter; we spoke on the phone. This is Grayson Moore."

The woman blushed. "It's alright Mr Carter; I know who Mr Moore is. I've had enough kids come through here now who love the Renegade films. Many despite the fact it has an age limit." She extended her hand to Grayson, and he shook it. "Please call me Judy; I'm Ash's foster mother. Come in, we are just finishing lunch. It is one of my kid's birthdays, so we have cake."

"It's lovely to meet you, Judy." Grayson stepped inside the door. "How many children do you have here?" He was genuinely interested in this angel of a woman.

"Five, Ash has been with me for eight months now. I was hoping that his mother would come for him, especially after I sent her the photo, but I heard nothing back. And then I saw the report about her suicide." He followed Judy through the house to the kitchen. Matthew was behind them. "He may be shy at first; I don't like to get the children's hopes up, so I only told him that a man was coming to do a test on him." Judy went to open the door, but he stopped her.

"Was he damaged?" The question was asked in a very shaky voice.

Judy placed her hand on his arm; the middle-aged woman gave him a reassuring smile. "Ash was lucky; I think the older girl helped look after him. She taught him to walk, talk everything that a baby needs. He was the youngest but had to grow up quickly. Those people." She spat out the word, "Hadn't even named him. He was called four because he was the fourth child. None of the children thought anything of that. When he came here and found the other kids had names we spent a lot of time deciding on one for him. We chose Ashkii because of his native looks. I can't believe that we got the right tribe. Fate I think. He is obviously behind in a lot of aspects, especially with his learning, but he goes to a pre-kindergarten here one day a week which has helped with his social ability. He is an adorable little boy, Mr Moore." She quieted and then opened the door. The noise of cheering and sounds of happy birthday being sung greeted him. He stepped into the room, and five pairs of eyes turned to face him. He only noticed one though. The ones that were the same as his. His breath hitched. Matthew stepped up behind him.

"You got this," Matthew stated supportingly.

"Hi everyone."

One of the older boys squealed; he guessed that the boy must be about fourteen. "It's Grayson Moore. Tilly, Judy got you Grayson Moore for your birthday."

The girl, Tilly, he assumed by the big birthday cake in front of her, jumped to her feet and ran to hug him. Her hugged her back. "Can you do that flip kick thing you do, that is so cool?"

"Tilly let Mr Moore go. I'm sure he'll do the kick for you later. He's had a long drive from LA, so let's get him a drink and a piece of your cake first.

"How far away is LA?" A boy of about eight asked.

"I would say about four hundred miles, I think," Grayson replied.

"Don't you know exactly?" The boy looked perturbed.

"I'll find out the exact miles for you later, Evan." Judy interrupted. "Evan is autistic; he likes to know exact details on things."

Matthew stepped forward and pulled his phone out, "I will Google it with him." He handed Grayson the DNA kit.

"Ashkii, why don't you come and sit next to Mr Moore?" The little boy looked up at Judy with his dark eyes.

"Is he the man who will do my test."

"He is honey."

The little boy slid off his chair and came to sit next to Grayson.

"It's nice to meet you, Mr Moore. I don't know your films. When the others talk about them, I always say I want to see them, but Judy always says in a year or so as I'm a bit young to watch them right now. But the others have told me the good parts."

"That's ok. So how old is Tilly?" He couldn't take his eyes off the little boy, his affection for the child was already ingrained into his heart. He knew then that he was leaving this building with him

"She's fifteen."

"A big girl."

"Yes."

"It's three-hundred and eighty-one miles, exactly, and it's taken them almost six hours and forty-seven minutes to drive here." Evan ecstatically called out.

"Such a long drive." Ash looked up at him.

"Don't tell Evan, but we got a helicopter most of the way, so it didn't take us that much time," Grayson whispered to the boy.

"You've got a helicopter?" The boy's eyes went wide.

"I do. You can go in it one day if you want."

"Can I?" Luxury had become standard for Grayson now; he didn't think much of it. It was a part of his lifestyle, but this boy, he'd had none of that. He hadn't even had clothes and food. His heart ached.

"Of course, you can."

"Judy says you have to do a test on me?"

"I do. Are you alright with that?" DNA didn't matter to Grayson at all, at that moment.

"I am. I have to open my mouth, and then you'll rub something against my cheek." Ash opened his mouth.

"Good boy." Grayson pulled the test out, took the swab, and wiped it around the kid's mouth. He placed it into a sealed container and handed it to Matthew when he appeared behind him.

"This is where being ex-MI5 comes in handy. I'll go speak to Jasper and have the results for you in half an hour."

"I already know the results," Grayson exclaimed as Matthew left the room.

"Alright, kids, who's for cake?" Judy called out and started to cut pieces. Ash waited quietly until he was passed a piece then devoured it in super speed.

"I want a paw patrol cake for my birthday." Ash splattered crumbs all over the table when he spoke.

"I don't know paw patrol. I'll have to look it up." It suddenly dawned on him that he didn't know the first thing about being a father. The house wasn't even set up for a family.

"It's brilliant. I want to be Chase when I grow up. He's the police officer."

"Maybe we can watch it together later?"

"It's not my day for watching what I want; because it's Tilly's day, she gets to choose."

"You have to take it in turns to watch the TV?" Grayson was confused.

"Miss Judy can only afford one, so we have to share. We can watch it tomorrow, but then I guess you won't be here." The boy looked down into the last crumbs of his cake. Grayson looked over to Judy; the helpful lady was watching them together. He could see that she had tears in her eyes.

"Tell me more about Paw Patrol. What other characters are there in it?"

The next half an hour passed in a flurry of information on talking dogs who had special vehicles. Grayson was actually excited and wanted to watch the show. It sounded like a kid's version of the Renegade films. Ash had moved onto his lap at some point, and Grayson had his arm around him. The other children disappeared to play with a new toy that Tilly received. It was a small karaoke machine, which allowed them to sing songs at the tops of their voices. The floor upstairs vibrated with the fun they were having. Judy was busy trying to tidy the kitchen. He could see that she held great affection for the children but was struggling financially. In the past, he had been accused of not helping those in need, but he was going to make sure that for the rest of her life this woman had what she needed to continue to help these children.

Matthew appeared at the door. Grayson tilted his head at him in question.

"Positive."

He let out a long breath. In his heart, he already knew what the the outcome would be, and it wouldn't have changed the decision he was about to make, but it was nice to have the confirmation.

"Ash?" The little boy looked up at him.

"You know the test that we did."

"Yes."

"That showed that I'm your daddy." Judy stopped her cleaning and came back to the table just in case Ash got upset.

"My daddy?" Ash frowned.

"Yes."

"Does that mean I can come and live with you in LA?" He could see the little boy's mind working behind his eyes. He hoped that whatever it was saying was good.

"What you like to?"

"Do you have a TV?"

"I have five."

"Five!" The little boy exclaimed and bounced up on his lap. "So I can watch Paw Patrol whenever it is on?"

"Yes, of course, you can?"

"What about Miss Judy?"

"What about her?"

"I'll miss her."

"Whenever you want to see her then you can. I'm going to buy Miss Judy a bigger house and all your friends their own TV so they can watch whatever they want." Judy gasped.

"Can you buy her house near yours?"

"If she wants to." Grayson looked at Judy who had tears streaming down her face. He smiled at her, and she brought her hands together in front of her in a gesture of thank you. "So do you think you like to come and live with me?"

"Um." He hesitated again.

"What is it?" Grayson asked.

"Do I have a mommy?"

How was he supposed to answer that one? Yes, she's dead, but you don't want to know her 'because she is the reason that you had to be in that place you grew up in. His thoughts turned to Sophie, his little one, his life, his love; she was at home alone. He'd asked her not to come here. He was still trying to work through his thoughts on her and what she'd done. Tears came to his eyes. He wished she was a part of what he was experiencing now. They should be doing this together. He had his answer.

"Yes, you do have a mommy. Her name is Sophie, and she is going to be so excited to meet you."

Ash wrapped his little arms across his broad chest. "Let's go home, daddy."

CHAPTER EIGHTEEN

Sophie

A watched phone never rings. That was certainly what was happening to Sophie. She had been staring at the phone for hours now and nothing. Maybe it was broken. That had to be it. She swiped it on and tested it with a call to the home phone. It rang. Damn it! It was working. Why was this taking so long? She opened the folder that Matthew had left with her on Ashkii; she was barely been able to read the words with the tears that she shed after learning what had happened to him. Any guilt she had for killing Sally Bridgewater evaporated. The woman was evil scum and deserved to burn in Hell. If she could kill her again, she would and make sure it was much more painful this time. Sophie picked up the photo of Ashkii; he was such a beautiful little boy. The spitting image of his father. How much he had suffered. She just wanted to hold him and help him. Who knew she had a maternal instinct, but for this little boy, it was on full display. She just hoped Grayson would allow her to be a part of their lives. When he left, things were still very much up in the air. He had saved her from the pit of depression she was falling into. He'd known what she had needed despite his fear at what she was involved in. She was in every way possible a full time submissive. He'd seen that and used it to his advantage.

The Butler appeared in front of her.

"Mrs Moore, your brother is here." James strode confidently into the room.

"James." She jumped to her feet and ran into his big burly arms.

"Hi, little sis." He embraced her back; tapping her back to check on how much weight she had lost. "You look a little bit better than you did on the call yesterday."

"Grayson and I worked through a couple of things."

James raised a disgusted eyebrow. "So Matthew told me. I hope you are applying the balm regularly today, and he did get that cut checked, didn't he?" He turned her to examine the small abrasion on her head.

"Yes, he had a doctor come and put a couple of stitches in it."

"It was an accident?" The protective big brother was asking this.

"Yes, it was an accident. Everything was consensual."

"Good, because you know I will have Matthew kill him if he ever hurt you without consent."

"I'm kinkier than I thought, but you knew that even if I didn't." She shrugged and laughed.

"I did not need to know that. I think I may bring up my plane food." He brought her to his chest again. "Have you heard from them since they went to San Francisco?"

"No. I'm getting a little worried."

"I'll phone Matthew." James pulled out his phone and called. He did not put the phone on speaker though. "Hi Matthew, I'm with Sophie. What is happening?"

Sophie listened to the one-sided conversation for any hints as to the state of her marriage and Grayson's relationship with his son. She could guess nothing from her evasive brother's side of the conversation though.

"I'll get her packed, and we'll be there in a few hours," James said into the phone.

Were they going somewhere? Where? Was it to meet Grayson?

"I managed to find my way here safely. I think we'll be alright without a bodyguard."

Matthew replied to James' comment, and Sophie could guess what that comment was.

"Alright. I'll take one. Jesus, you are worse than Amy and Sonia. I'm a grown man; I think I've proven I can take care of myself on enough occasions."

Matthew repeated something, which she couldn't catch.

"That was one time; I got confused because I was tired. At least I had a nice few days' relaxation in the Maldives instead of working hard in India."

This time she caught most of the reply which was full of expletives.

"I said I was sorry for not telling you. There is no need to bitch at me again." James laughed. "I'll see you in a few hours." Her brother hung up and put his phone back into his jeans' pocket.

"By the end of today, I'm going to have no idea what time zone I'm in. You're lucky I love you, little sis."

"We're going somewhere?"

"Yep."

"Where?" Her tone was maybe a little too impatient.

"To meet your husband and son in Navajo Nation."

CHAPTER NINETEEN

Grayson

"Shimá, Shizhé'é" Grayson called out for his parents when he walked through the door of their home. His heart had told him that this was the first place that he needed to bring the boy.

"Giní." His mother replied and raced out of the kitchen. She stopped dead when she saw the little boy beside him. His father appeared beside his mother and caught her when she began to fall, having fainted at the surprise.

"Mom." He stepped forward and helped to assist her to a chair. Ashkii remained where he was just looking around the big house. Grayson motioned for him to join them.

"How, when, I...?" The torrent of questions tumbled from his mother's lips.

"I'll explain that later but first, Ashkii." His son stepped forward and wrapped his arms around Grayson's legs. He was nervous. "I want you to meet your grandparents."

"Hello." He stuttered nervously.

"Hello." They both replied. His mother was sobbing.

"Giní, I can't believe this?"

"He's mine, mom." His son looked up at him.

"Why does Nanna call you Giní?" His mom whimpered a little happiness at the use of an affectionate term for her.

"That is my native name. It mean's Hawk."

"Mine means boy." He said proudly.

"It does. We'll teach you lots of our language." Grayson's father responded.

"I can't wait." Ash let go of his leg and went to his grandfather's arms. "Thank you, Grandpa."

Matthew coughed in the doorway.

"Sorry to interrupt. Swan is outside, and she's not saying

the most pleasant things about you. I didn't think your parents would appreciate me hog-tying and gagging her to shut her up, so I figured it best that I tell you."

His mother let out a little cry of shock at the bodyguard's blunt words.

"That was an excellent idea. Mom, will you look after Ash for me."

"Giní, let your father speak to her, please."

"No, I need to put an end to her tainting of me. It has to stop." He was a father now; he was a husband, a good person, and he wasn't going to let his sister's warped views run him out of his ancestral home. He would always support his family, promote his culture. Yes, he had lost his way, but he was home again now.

"Daddy." Ash was at his side.

"Yes."

"You're coming back?" He got down onto his haunches in front of Ash. The fear in the little boy's eyes ripped at his heart.

"I'm just going to be outside for a little while. You stay with Nanna and Grandpa, and then, when I come back, I'll take you to meet the Chiefs. Would you like that?"

"Yes, please. Do they have the big hats that Evan said they do?"

"They do, and if you are a very good boy, I'm sure that they will let you wear one."

"Can I, can I? I promise that I'll be good."

"Of course."

"Ash." His mother came and took the boy's hand. "Why don't you come in the kitchen with me. I made cake earlier. Shall we get you a piece?"

"Two pieces of cake in one day. I can't believe it." Ash and his grandmother disappeared off into the kitchen. Grayson's father stepped forward. "I think I've been too lax with Swan."

"It's not your fault dad. Swan is independent and feisty. She has a role on the Council and uses it."

"A lot like her mother was until I married her. Maybe that is what is needed to mellow Swan."

"Heaven help the poor guy." Grayson laughed. He helped his father out of the house by holding the door open. They went to the courtyard outside the front of the building. A large crowd had gathered. Swan stood on the bonnet of his car preaching her sermon.

"Another visit, two years we heard nothing from him. That article is published, and he is here all the time. This time, he comes with a child who looks just like him." How had Swan known about that? Grayson looked around and saw his parents' neighbour amongst the throng of people. She gave him a smug smirk. Eyes everywhere. "That child is the product of the ways he fell into. The ways that are not of our people. He does not show any respect to us to bring that thing here."

Matthew cracked his knuckles next to them.

"It's alright. She'll come out of this looking the fool."

"You sure I can't gag her?"

Grayson shook his head.

Swan continued, "If that thing is indeed our blood, then, we need to rescue it from him. Mould the child to our culture. Get it away from its father's materialistic nature. The money appears now for fixing up the community centre, and Gini with it. Photo shoots in magazines to show what he does help his family. But that is only because I took a stand and did that article. Showed the world who he truly is. His club is destroyed; the angry people of Los Angeles burnt it down. They don't want him, and neither do we. Grayson Moore is the devil. I say we ban him from the Navajo Nation. Cast him out forever. Who is with me?"

A few cheers went up, and several of them looked around at him chanting 'Out, Out, Out'.

"I think I've heard enough. Time to put this crowd right." Before he could push his way through the crowd to the front, a tiny figure, that he instantly recognised, stepped forward. Sophie jumped onto the bonnet and pushed Swan off.

"Swan has had her say; now, I get mine."

CHAPTER TWENTY

Sophie

Sophie couldn't believe what she was hearing. The world was full of delusional women when it came to her husband. He'd made mistakes in the past, they both had, but they were good people. Grayson had never forgotten his culture; it was a part of him. It was always there. James tried to drag her into the house, but she was having none of it. Swan had had her say on her brother; it was Sophie's turn to now defend her husband. She pushed James off her and jumped up onto the car. Swan had quickly toppled from the bonnet with a firm shove.

"Swan has had her say, and no I get mine." The crowd quieted. Shocked at her sudden appearance, a few started to heckle her, but she silenced them with a stare. "You are good people and need to hear both sides of the story. I know that you will listen."

A hush fell over the crowd. Swan was up on her feet to protest, but her father appeared by her side, and Sophie heard him tell her to be quiet. She looked up, and Grayson stood next to his father. She wanted to run to him, but he gestured for her to continue. She coughed to clear her throat.

"I know what a lot of you think of Giní; he was seduced by the fame and fortune. That I'm nothing but a slave to him. He mistreats women and couldn't care less about his heritage, but none of you know the man who I love." She raised her voice even higher. "He is a kind and caring husband. Yes, we don't have a traditional relationship. I'm a twenty-four-hour submissive to him. That means that he dresses me, feeds me, and if I'm naughty punishes me. But that doesn't mean he treats me like a slave or a child. I'm a grown woman. I make decisions myself. I'm a successful PA; I manage his career. I have a brain. All our relationship means is that I trust him. I trust him in ways that not everybody will understand. I know that when I fall apart, he will be there to put me back together." She looked down at Grayson, and he placed his hand over his heart and mouthed always. As if it was the confirmation that she needed that he still loved her, she tried desperately to fight back the tears.

"I've lived with Giní for a long time now. The first meal I had with him was Goat's milk pancakes. I was hooked; and whenever I want them, he makes them for me. Most of the food that we eat originates from recipes that he learnt when growing up here. When he wakes in the morning, the first thing that he does is pray to the Sun God. He spent ages teaching me the incantations, and I join him as well. The native culture has entwined with mine. Our home is full of indigenous artefacts that he has rescued from being sold off to foreign buyers to be lost forever. We have a room that we painted with just symbols of your culture. We sing and dance to Navaho music. We buy rugs from those woven with loving care by the people who we meet. I know that we have not visited as much as we have wanted to, in the past few years and that I took him away from you all to England to marry him. I wish in some ways I could have combined the two cultures more, but I was the selfish one and wanted the princess wedding I'd dreamed of since a little girl. Grayson, Giní, is not to blame for that. All he did was give me what I wanted."

The crowd had fallen quiet around them. Several of the women were crying as well.

"I don't deny that he went through a wild phase. Neither would he. LA is a city that does that to you. I've not met the little boy, yet, but yes, he brought his son here to meet his grandparents." She hoped Grayson didn't mind her admitting that they'd still not had a chance to discuss everything or anything. The big smile he still had on his face said that he was not angry. "We did not know of the child until recently, and the second Giní knew, he went straight to find the boy and bring him home." Her voice broke again. "Home as in here, Navajo, not LA. He brought Ashkii back to his people. If he were ashamed or wanted to forget his heritage, he would not have done that. We would be in LA and not here to show you a new member of your family. He does value his ancestry; he wants to help you all. He wants to help everyone. A large part of Grayson's income is donated to projects around LA, and though he has been remiss in seeing that his donations reached his tribe in the past, he is ensuring that now." She wrapped her arms around her body. "If, after the things I have just said, you still want to ban him from his home then we will leave, but we will take his son with us and ensure that he is taught all about his culture and heritage. Even if he cannot visit it. Thank you for listening to me." She went to the edge of the car and jumped down into Grayson's arms. He brought his lips down to hers and kissed her as though he had been starved of her sweetness for eternity.

"I love you." He whispered into her ear when they parted.

"Forever." She replied.

A massive cheer went up in the crowd. They were calling Hawk. "What's happening?" She asked

"I think my people have decided they want me to stay." Grayson smiled.

"They are idiots; you will betray them again." Swan stood up to her brother.

"He never betrayed them in the first place; you did when you did that article." Sophie didn't like her sister-in-law.

"Swan, I think it is time to let your jealousy of your brother go." Grayson's father interjected.

"Jealous. I'm not jealous."

"Hush. Enough. I think it is time that you learnt about the real world. Now we have a grandchild, we are going to be spending a lot more time in LA, and you can join us.

Who knows? We may even find you a husband to shut you up."

"Dad."

"Don't dad me. You may be on the Council, but family comes first."

"Fine." Swan stomped off like a petulant teenager.

"She'll sulk for a few days, and then we'll talk to her again. The people have spoken, and you are part of the family again, son." Grayson and his father embraced, slapping each other on the backs. Some of the other people, who had been in the crowd, came up and congratulated Grayson on becoming a father, saying they couldn't wait to meet the boy, and he must join them for supper soon.

Matthew handed her a tissue to wipe away the tears.

"Thank you, Matthew."

"You're welcome Mrs Moore."

"So where is my nephew then." James was there beside her.

"Nephew."

Grayson took Sophie's hands.

"We may have to make a decision to tell Ashkii the truth in the future, but he asked me today if he had a mommy. I said that it was you. He can't wait to meet you." She looked at him with her mouth open.

"Grayson. I. I can't. What I did. I killed his mother." She didn't deserve to be a mother to that boy.

"You killed a vile piece of garbage who didn't not deserve to be called a woman let alone a mother. She lost any right to that boy when she chose a newspaper article over him. You did him a favour."

"Are you sure?" She was holding onto a little bit of hope.

"Let's go meet your son."

The group dispersed, and she took Grayson's hand. Matthew and James followed them. When they got to the door, it opened, and Ashkii came running out. He was so much like Grayson that she instantly fell in love with him.

"Mommy." He called and jumped straight into her arms.

"Daddy said that you were on your way. You're so pretty."

She had a lump the size of Texas in her throat.

"I think Mommy is very happy to see you." Grayson took the little boy from her. "You're still weak; I don't want you to exert yourself too much." That wouldn't stop her from wrapping her arms around them both though.

"Yes, Master." She bit her lip at the use of the normal word for Grayson.

"Why did you call him Master?" Ash asked.

James and Matthew chuckled behind them.

"I think these two are going to have a swift introduction to having a child around."

Sophie glared at them. "It's just a term of affection for him." Parenting 101 success. She stuck her tongue out at her brother.

"Master, can we have some more cake please?" Ash asked his father.

Sophie and Grayson looked at each other and burst out laughing. It was a Parenting 101 fail.

CHAPTER TWENTY-ONE

Grayson

"I never realised how energetic a five-year-old boy could be." Sophie collapsed onto the bed in Grayson's parents' spare room.

"He's certainly going to keep us on our toes."

Sophie sat up and wrapped her arms around his shoulders while he removed his shoes.

"I like it but are you sure about him calling me mummy."

"Never surer. If we have to tell him about Sally, we will, but I want him to know that he is loved by the two of us."

"He certainly is." He suspected his wife was as in love with the little munchkin as much as he was. "We'll have to change the dynamic of our relationship."

"Why?"

"Er...how would you explain to him me eating my dinner off the floor for example." She raised an eyebrow at him. That was true. Could they still have a twenty-four-seven submissive relationship with a five-year-old child living with them? Why couldn't they? As long as they gave him a healthy appreciation for women as equals and explained the relationship minus the sex bits; because he would never be ready for that at such a tender age, they could be as they always had been. Ok, Sophie would have typically eaten her dinner naked; that may have to change, but the essential elements of their relationship didn't have to.

"I would tell him that mommy had been naughty and she needed to think about what she had done. It's no different to us telling him off when he has been naughty."

"You do realise that he may ask why daddy never gets to eat on the floor."

"Because daddy is never naughty." He retorted with a

chuckle.

"Mommy begs to differ on that. I think he's very naughty in the playroom sometimes."

"Only when I need to be." He twisted her around and laid her out on his lap. "I owe you an apology. I was going to walk out of a scene without any aftercare."

"Don't" She reached up and pressed her fingers to his lips.

"No." He kissed them and pulled them away. "This needs to be said. What happened between us was very intense. You didn't mention a safe word. I just need to check that you are alright with it."

She entwined her hand with his and brought it down to rest on her breast through the sleeveless top she wore.

"You saved me that day. I was drowning. I'd become someone who wasn't faithful to her beliefs. You brought me back. It's what I always trusted you to do. To know what I need better than I know myself. That is the dynamic of our relationship. So to answer your question, yes, I'm alright with everything that happened."

He leant down and kissed her. It felt like forever since they had been like this.

"I was thinking. My parents have a lot of lands out back. I'm going to ask them if we can build a place on some of it. Nothing fancy, just a place we can bring Ash and stay every now and then."

"I was thinking as well." She laughed, "We live in the modern world. Communication with everyone is secure via a computer or phone. We don't need to be in LA all the time. Why don't we make our permanent home here? What Ash needs more than anything now is family."

"Are you serious?" He didn't think that she'd want to leave LA, to immerse herself even more in his culture. He'd made enough money to last a lifetime and then some. He didn't need to work all the time. He wanted to spend more time at home with Ash and Sophie. Maybe even take a turn on the Council.

"Yes, this is where we belong. I still want to go to LA; a lady needs clothes, and once the club is repaired, we have to scene in it again. But I feel happy and content here; more than that, I feel free."

"I better talk to your brother in the morning then. Get him started on drawing up the plans."

Sophie sat up on his lap.

"Master, will you make love to me?" He studied her, not saying a word. "You are making me self-conscious now." She shivered.

"No words." He replied before pulling her top over her head. He removed her bra and nestled in between her breasts. Slowly, he took one nipple into his mouth and sucked it to a hard peak. He then repeated the same with the other one. "Perfection."

She laughed and wiggled her bottom over his hardening cock. "Perfection."

"You know what naughty little subs get don't you?"

"A spanking." She looked hopeful.

"Normally, but I'm afraid you will still be too sore after the paddle. So for tonight you just get this."

He picked her up and threw her onto the bed. She squealed. He was going to have to gag her. Damn it. He didn't have his bag with him. The belt of his jeans would have to do. He pulled it through the loops of his trousers while Sophie watched from under hooded eyes. She knew what was coming, and he bet she was practically dripping wet inside her shorts. He looped the belt around her face and brought it down to rest over her mouth. "That should keep you a little quieter. The whole Navajo Nation doesn't really need to hear you screaming my name."

She grumbled behind the belt.

"You tap me twice on the left shoulder to stop everything or even anything." It was something they had worked out before during play where she could not speak openly. She tapped him once on the right shoulder. This was her confirmation that she understood. "There is something that

I've really missed recently, and that is the taste of your succulent pussy. I bet you are wet for me already aren't you, little one? Are you ready to accept your Master's tongue?" He licked his lips while undoing her shorts and pulling them down her legs. Her tiny panties followed. He sniffed them. "Sweet as always but with an added element of danger. I think it makes you even more delectable. And indeed more fuckable, not that my dick ever wants to leave your pussy." The dirty talk was flying from his mouth tonight. It had been so long since they had been able to just be Sophie and Grayson. They'd allowed others to interfere in their relationship. It had brought them to the point of destruction, but they survived it and were stronger than ever. His woman parted her legs for him, and he nearly came in his pants. She was dripping for him. The aroma was heady. He buried his head between her thighs. Her naked sex open and waiting for him. He used his fingers to unfurl her labia and went straight for her clit, teasing it, tantalising it, drawing it from its hiding place. She was his favourite meal, and he would worship it every day forever. He eased a finger inside her. She must have been sore from the other day. They had been very rough, and he didn't want this to cause he any more discomfort

"More." She mumbled around the leather gag. His goddess had spoken; he gave her what she wanted. He curled his two fingers, which were inside her, up to stroke at the sensitive spot within her. He could hammer nails with his cock it was that hard, but this was about Sophie. About his job as a Dominant to take her trust and reward her for it. He flicked over her clit again, and she came, washing his face with her essence. He licked up every last drop. He would never get enough. He pulled his fingers out, and she groaned at the empty feeling.

"I will make you feel full again soon."

He pushed off the bed and dropped his jeans and pants. His cock sprang out. It was fiercely ready for taking Sophie. But tonight wasn't about fucking, it was about making love.

It was about showing his wife that he adored her, and they would be a fire together. He sat on the bed with his legs out in front of him.

"Come here." She obeyed and knelt before him. "I want you to sit on my cock and then place your bottom on the bed." She had to still be sore from the paddle so having her on his legs would hurt her bottom. "Put your legs over my shoulders and join your feet behind the back of my head. I'll do the rest." Sophie settled herself exactly as he'd asked. When she slid onto him, he let out a loud moan of pleasure. Maybe he should have gagged himself as well. This was his wife, and he was worried about his parents hearing them making love. The sooner he got the house built, the better.

"This is going to be a slow burn little one. I want to watch you as we make love. I want to see the moment that my cock hits the parts inside you that make you come. I want to look at you as your pussy clenches down on my cock and milks me for all I can give you." Sophie had tears in her eyes again. He didn't want her gagged for this. He wanted this natural. Just the two of them joined together. He dropped her legs and reached around to remove the leather belt.

"I might scream." She whispered.

"Scream all you want. I'm not ashamed of what we do."

He started to rock his hips, and Sophie pushed against the bed in perfect rhythm with him. They were slowly moving themselves to orgasm. He lifted his head to take her lips. Seal the love and affection that they had for each other. Their tongues twisted in a passionate tango; sweat glistened over their bodies in a beautiful sheen of arousal. They were moving as man and wife, as two lovers who were moving as one, who were one in ecstasy. They both pulled back from the kiss as they felt their combined climaxes approaching. He held her ardent stare, neither of them blinked as simultaneously he thrust in one final time and gave her everything he had while she clenched down on him and bathed him with her love.

He pulled her down beside him. He would stay inside her, as long as he could, as long as he stayed hard and long.

He never understood the actual value of heritage until this moment and the need to control it and hold it close. Heritage was the past, present, and more importantly, the future. It was in him. It was in Sophie. It was in Ashkii. It was what defined them, guided them, and guarded them. What he and Sophie did together would leave a legacy for generations to come. The Navajo people worshipped the natural; they embraced it and nurtured it. He had been blinded by the materialistic. He'd forgotten his true roots, and it had taken the tragedy to return him home. But now he was here, he would never leave again. For he had his wife, his son, and his family by his side.

Ryan

He watched the wooden coffin lowered into the ground. He wasn't going to shed any tears for this malevolent woman. He knew that she was planning to double cross him and had already started planning her story. Sally Bridgewater lived for a story, and she died for it as far as he was concerned. She wasn't a pleasant woman, and Grayson Moore had fallen into her trap because of his overactive libido.

He watched the few mourners dressed in black over coats, to protect against the coming cold of winter, throw their handfuls of dirt on top of the black coffin. She was in Hell now. Just where she belonged in the fiery pit of pain. She made a good toy for the Devil. He rejoiced that he had put her there. Sophie really wasn't the most intelligent of the North siblings; he guessed that came from her over whelming need to have everything done for her. She was a child who had never grown up. He was there that day and listened to the entire conversation between the two women. She even walked past him hidden in the shadows when she left the room where Sally fell. It presented him with the perfect opportunity. He went in just as Sally came back to consciousness. She tried to get up, but he held her down and cut off her ability to breath until she spluttered her last breath in his arms. He had to be careful. Matthew Carter was on his way. The bodyguard was ex-MI5 and was trained to know if something was wrong. He made sure it looked like Sally died from the head wound. It wasn't as if they were going to do an autopsy to diagnose the cause of death. Not in the current location she was in anyway. James North was that obvious and controlling. He would do anything to protect his sister, and that had played right into his hands.

He left the graveyard with the other mourners. Exchanging pleasantries and saying inconsolable condolences for the tragic loss as he went. This was the part of his job that he loved; tying up the loose end towards the finale. His time was coming; he would have his revenge. Years of wondering why he was cast aside had twisted him into the bitter shell that he was today. Nothing made sense. Why him? What was wrong with him? What was so special about James and Sophie North anyway. They were rich kids who thought they could get away with anything. Well, the stack of evidence was mounting against them. Everything they knew would soon crumble.

He climbed into his black saloon car, paid for by his highly skilled job, with all the latest gadgets. They meant nothing to him except a means to an end. He tapped a button on his dashboard and a touch screen computer screen popped up. With a press of his thumb to the screen, two faces he knew well appeared on it. His mother and father. Not that they deserved that loving title. Not after what they had done to him. Abandoned him for no apparent reason. He stroked his mother's smiling face. He saw elements of himself in her, the slight wave at the corner of his mouth. The green hue that tinted his eyes. However, it was his father who he resembled more. His well built structure, his square jawline, and the set of his eyes. Thankfully, prosthetics hid that most of the time. They'd even made him hate his own face. That was how much they damaged him with their rejection. He pushed the screen away and started the engine.

Thanks to Sally Bridgewater, he had the evidence to destroy his brother and sister and all their friends. James, Sophie, and their families would have nothing in this world, just like him. The world would see them all for the monster's they really were. The people who controlled all around them on the belief that they had the right to murder and defile. All he needed for his revenge was the final pieces of the puzzle to crush his parents. He was ready to demand answers to so many unanswered questions that he had. Miranda and Pete North's time on planet Earth was limited. Death was coming and he would bathe in their blood.

THE END

The Control Series continues with
Michael and Collette's story soon.

Plus look out for Alexia and Andrei's story in the
Author Friends with Benefits Anthology
to be released at Christmas 2017.

The Control Series: A dramatic, witty, and sensual suspense romance set predominantly in London.

Surrendered Control, The Control Series, Book 1:
Amazon US http://amzn.to/2gDAgtG
Amazon UK http://amzn.to/2gGShn5
Goodreads http://bit.ly/2fOdQEK

Divided Control, The Control Series, Book 2:
Amazon US http://amzn.to/2gutKT7
Amazon UK http://amzn.to/2gDqV58
Goodreads http://bit.ly/2gdtMhv

Misguided Control, The Control Series, Book 3:
AmazonUK: http://amzn.to/2lxiqM0
Amazon US: http://amzn.to/2lxojca
Goodreads: http://bit.ly/2rEaxa5

Controlling Darkness, The Control Series, Book 4:
AmazonUK: http://amzn.cu/22w00DN
Amazon US: http://a.co/85CKiOa
Goodreads: http://bit.ly/2sr4ogP

Controlling Heritage, The Control Series, Book 5:
AmazonUK: http://amzn.eu/22w00DN
Amazon US: http://a.co/85CKiOa
Goodreads: http://bit.ly/2sr4ogP

PARNORMAL ROMANCE BOOKS BY ANNA EDWARDS

The Glacial Blood world is full of intrigue, suspense and kick arse fights. It also features a secret that should remain untold. A family isn't always blood; it's the people in your life that accept you for what you are.

The Touch of Snow, The Glacial Blood Series, Book 1:
Amazon US http://amzn.to/2tNQd2W
Amazon UK http://amzn.to/2tO6t43
iBooks http://apple.co/2uiVBNv
Goodreads http://bit.ly/2gQQQre

Fighting the Lies, The Glacial Blood Series, Book 2:
Coming October 2017

Dear Reader,

I hope you enjoyed this book. I'd love it if you could post a review about it on Amazon and Goodreads. Getting reviews for my books is such a thrill as it allows me to see what readers enjoy or even, dislike about what I write. It's all good for me to learn. Perhaps you could mention which is your favourite character and what parts you like best. You could also say which character you're looking forward to reading more about in a new book.

If you've spotted a typo, email me at
anna1000edwards@gmail.com.

I look forward to hearing from you.

Anna Edwards

PS – Read on for a preview of my new paranormal series!

A new series from international author Anna Edwards,
The Glacial Blood Series, a paranormal romance series.

The barren desert wasteland with its hues of gold, orange, and red sped past the car window. The rock formations were a testament to years of erosion beaten down by forces greater than he could understand. As a shape-shifting snow leopard, Brayden Dillon knew a lot about the ways of Mother Nature. Considering he spent most of his time exploring the snow-capped peaks of The Glacial National Park he already had the air-conditioning turned up as high as it would go. The brand-new Ford Mustang he drove had been a gift from his Alpha, Kas, in recognition for a job done well. So was the break from duties as pack Enforcer. Why his mother had to live just outside Death Valley was beyond him. You really couldn't get a hotter place on Earth. She'd told him it was because his father had always lived in the snow. When he died, she decided to get some sun. She hadn't looked back.

He pulled his Mustang up outside the café and shut off the roar of the high-powered engine. The disapproving looks from the locals soon vanished when he climbed out of the car. His height of six foot five silenced any potential disagree-ment. He purred to himself in contentment, but that was quickly lost when the heat of the midday sun hit him. He was not designed for this weather. He had all the usual snow leop-ard attributes: thick black hair with smoky gray flecks, small ears, and big feet that helped with bal-ance. He was pale be-cause he rarely spent time sunbathing like the lions and tigers in his pack. Dusk to dawn was when he was the most active. He made quick steps towards the café and into the air-conditioned building.

He didn't see his mother, only a fresh-faced waitress. She wore the café's uniform--a barely-there skirt and a tank top that was almost a second skin. She was pretty, in a timid sort of way. Every time someone came near her she flinched, and he could smell her fear. Well, he assumed it was fear. His judgment was slightly clouded by the fact that he needed a drink, preferably ice cold and dumped over his head. She ap-proached the seat he had taken near the counter.

"Hi. Welcome to the Last Stop. I'm Selene, and I'll be your waitress today. Can I get you an ice water to start with? It sure is a hot one out there today." Any sign of her nerves had dis-appeared, replaced with a business-like smile.

"Yes please, lots of ice. In fact, just bring me a big bowl of ice."

She laughed, her tiny nose crinkling up and dimples ap-pearing in her cheeks. Up close, she was even prettier than he'd originally thought. "Let me guess." She took a step back and looked him up and down. "Well, the fact you seem as if you're melting, I take it you're not a southerner. The lack of a tan confirms that but I can't quite place the accent?"

"Montana."

"No wonder you're hot. I'll bring you ice cream as well." She spun around in her little ballet pumps and started to stride off. Something stopped her. She turned back and took another long look at him; an eyebrow raising in question. "Brayden?"

ABOUT ANNA EDWARDS

Anna Edwards is a British Author that has a love of travelling and developing plot lines for stories. She has spent that last two years learning the skills of writing after being an Accountant since the age of 21. As well as Roleplaying on twitter, she can also be found writing poetry on twitter under the account,
Jane @harmoniccascade.

Her debut novel, Surrendered Control was released in November 2016 and has received fantastic feedback on the drama of story.

In her writing she loves to combine her love for romantic and erotic novels with her passion for travel to give an international feel to her novels. Yorkshire, she travelled to with friends recently and was captured by the beauty of it and the kindness of the locals.

For her tenth wedding anniversary, she travelled to The Wynn with her husband. While they didn't exactly hit the high rollers room they enjoyed the experience of being treated like royalty.

CONNECT WITH ANNA EDWARDS

www.AuthorAnnaEdwards.com

Facebook, Author Page: AnnaEdwardsWriter

Facebook, Friend: TheAuthorAnnaEdwards

Twitter: @Anna__Edwards

Instagram: authorannaedwards

Pinterest: anna1000edwards

Goodreads: anna__edwards

Bookbub: https://www.bookbub.com/authors/anna-edwards

Email: anna1000edwards@gmail.com

Made in the USA
Columbia, SC
18 January 2018